# First

# Year

# Varsity

*Time Spent in the Lost and Found*

Mary Marino

INFINITY
PUBLISHING

Copyright © 2010 by Mary Marino

ISBN 978-0-7414-6192-6

Printed in the United States of America

This is a work of fiction. Names, characters, places, and incidents either are the product of the author's imagination or are used fictitiously. Any resemblance to actual events or locales or persons, living or dead, is entirely coincidental.

Published December 2011

INFINITY PUBLISHING
1094 New DeHaven Street, Suite 100
West Conshohocken, PA 19428-2713
Toll-free (877) BUY BOOK
Local Phone (610) 941-9999
Fax (610) 941-9959
Info@buybooksontheweb.com
www.buybooksontheweb.com

To Friends Found –

We may dive into the competition alone,

but if we're lucky

we emerge at the end with some friends.

And if we hit the jackpot,

they remain by our side for a lifetime.

# - 1 -

"Jackie … Jackie McKendry, wake up!"

The words short-circuited my dream and images of winning goals and cheering crowds came skidding to a stop. I mumbled something about summer vacation and pulled the pillow over my head.

Apparently 'the voice' didn't like my attitude and began shaking my shoulder.

"You didn't set the alarm. Remember what day it is!"

Suddenly it hit me. My eyes flew open to find my mom standing over me looking mighty annoyed. I tried to avoid her stare, glancing instead to the calendar above my desk where a big red star marked the day. A smile crossed my face. I had been waiting all summer — the first day of field hockey camp!

I felt a rush of adrenaline kick me into high gear and began to snatch up the clothes laid out so carefully the night before. I guess it was a sign to my mom that I was up 'for real.' She left the room shaking her head, probably wondering if I was ready to go to an overnight camp if I couldn't even remember to set an alarm clock.

I could see my excitement as I wiped the steam from the bathroom mirror. But as I leaned closer I noticed something else. It was nerves. This was a camp for high school teams, and it wasn't just us sophomores from Northfield High that were going. Our school's upperclassmen would be there, too, and these were the girls that had put us through a dangerous hazing when we were freshmen. I wondered if the older girls hated us as much as they seemed to a year ago.

"Jackie, get moving! We should have been at the twins' house by now," Mom called, referring to my two best buds who were going to camp with me.

I quickly put thoughts of the upperclassmen behind me and scrounged around in a drawer for a ponytail holder. Securing my wild curls up into a short knot on top of my head, I peered into the mirror and frowned. I knew I needed to wear my hair up for camp, but it made me look so young — like that baby Pebbles from the Flintstones cartoons.

I wondered for a moment if the coaches at camp would take one look at me and tell me I should go play in the sandbox and not try to mix it up with the big girls.

*        *        *

My parents were waiting as I slid into the back seat of the car. I didn't even get a chance to bite into my breakfast bar before my mom turned around wearing one of those parent faces that snare you with their silent intensity. Adults must stand in front of the mirror and practice those looks for hours before they're even allowed to have children. It was my mom's 'you **do** have everything, don't you?' face. I nodded and crossed my fingers, just in case.

My dad had barely put the car into park when I leaped out and raced up the steps to the Hanson twins' house.

"You pumped, or what?" I asked when Jules Hanson answered the door.

She laughed. "Come on in. Tori's still getting dressed. She doesn't exactly pop right up in the morning."

The sound of footsteps on the stairs caused me to turn. It was Jules' identical twin, making her not-so-grand entrance. Her eyes were like slits and her hair spilled out of her ponytail in a dozen different directions.

"Maybe going to this camp is not the way to start sophomore year," Tori grumbled. "I just want to go back to bed," she said as she collapsed onto the bottom step.

Jules rolled her eyes, like, 'how can we possibly be related?' Tori caught it and told her to cut it out. I grinned at their bickering. As usual it didn't amount to much. Whenever things did heat up between the twins, they never forced me to take sides. This made being their friend a heck of a lot easier.

While I was fair and on the small side, the twins had their mother's dark, Italian coloring and their father's height. Some of our friends could get intimidated by them 'cause the twins had a real take-charge attitude. Once you met their parents you could see why. Their dad was this hotshot basketball coach at St. Benedict's Prep and Mrs. Hanson owned her own consulting business. But none of that stuff bothered me and I considered myself darn lucky the day they moved to town.

The twins were still going at it, so I went back outside only to have my mom jump on me as soon as she saw me coming out the door.

"Jackie, make sure you have everything out of the back of the car," she said, as she looked up from her conversation with my dad and Mr. Hanson.

To pacify her I pulled out my crumpled 'to pack' list from my back pocket and gave the car one more look. I waved the paper like I had it all under control and saw her mouth kind of tighten up.

I guess she wasn't impressed. To be fair, I was a real goof-ball, almost messing up my whole hockey career last year forgetting stuff. Still, my mom should have realized I was all grown up, making lists for everything now. Mothers were probably the last to know how mature you really were.

My parents gave me a quick hug goodbye. They were anxious to get an early start for the shore to pick up my little sister, Lizzie, and wanted to beat the bumper-to-bumper traffic. My sister had been at our grandma's beach house all week, probably being spoiled rotten, something everyone over the age of eighteen liked to do since the day she was born. It's not like I'm really complaining. Ever since Lizzie arrived, the pressure was off me to be Mom's little princess.

Sometimes my mom didn't know what to make of me being a tomboy and all. Sports were **so** not her. When I was little, she tried to priss me up, but somewhere along the line I put my foot down, and the dresses came flying off and the ribbons disappeared from my hair. So, I was relieved that Lizzie was a girly-girl, and hoped that Mom would eventually give up and let me be me.

This week my mom and I were kind of in 'truce' mode, but life with us was always a moment-to-moment roller-coaster kind of thing. And, as I watched my parents drive away, I wondered if my mom secretly wished I was going to a week of charm school instead of hockey camp.

\*　　\*　　\*

The sound system in Mr. Hanson's cushy town car soon put the twins to sleep, but I was too jazzed for napping. Gazing out the window, South Jersey seemed like one big suburb. Occasionally I'd see an open field and stretches of water surrounded by lots of scrub pines. I don't know if anyone would call it pretty, like in a painting or postcard, but it was home, and that was good enough for me.

After a time my mind started to wander and images of my boyfriend, Mitch Kennedy, came drifting through my head. Unlike Tori, who broke the freshman record for her number of boyfriends, Mitch and I had been together most all of freshman year. Of course maybe Mitch and I were only technically still together since I hadn't seen him all summer.

In June he had gone back to Texas to be with his mom and two sisters. Two months was a long time to be apart and I wondered if he'd feel the same about me when he came back to New Jersey to spend the school year with his dad.

More than once last year, I had caught girls drooling over him with claws only slightly hidden. Lucky for me he hadn't noticed. But maybe things had changed in Texas. All I knew was — I missed him a lot.

"Pit stop," Mr. Hanson called out as we pulled into the Turnpike service plaza.

Inside the Welcome Center, the twins and I bumped into two girls coming out of the restroom wearing Northfield field hockey shirts. I figured they were upperclassmen since I didn't know them. They looked at the three of us like we were from outer space, but I was sure they had to recognize the twins 'cause they were kind of hard to miss.

"Oh, hi, are you all going to camp, too?" one of the girls asked, like she just noticed us.

The girl sounded like she really didn't care where we were going, but she couldn't exactly ignore us. We were right in her path. When we introduced ourselves, she barely gave me a glance. Instead she zeroed in on the twins.

"I'm Bri and this is Allison. We're seniors," she said.

"How many of us will there be from Northfield?" Jules asked.

"Coach said there would be twenty-five," Allison, who'd been eyeing a display of sunglasses, said.

I blinked. I hadn't expected so many.

"Yeah, it's a lot of competition for you guys," Bri said, like she was above it all and had her place locked up. She looked at the other girl. "We better go, Allie. See ya," she said, brushing by us.

Walking back to the car Tori said, "Why do I have the feeling that some people haven't gotten over last year?"

Jules gave her sister a grim smile.

"Is this going to be a long week?" I asked, thinking about all the ways the upperclassmen could make our lives miserable.

"It's going to be a fun week. We're going to make sure of it," Jules said.

I couldn't tell if she really believed this or if Jules was just determined that things would be okay. For a moment attending this camp didn't seem to be such a great idea and I wondered if Mr. Hanson would be willing to switch me to a round-trip ticket for home.

# - 2 -

The university, where camp was being held, was overwhelming. It was like a whole city. There were even high rises and buildings bigger than my whole elementary school. I wondered how anyone could find their way to class. It would take forever.

*Suppose I get lost and get to the fields late. They'd probably make me do sprints.*

Waiting in the check-in line, my anxiety level grew. When the registration lady handed Jules her papers we discovered she was the only Northfield player in her group. She seemed okay with it, but I would have been miserable being with a bunch of strangers.

As Tori picked up her papers I noticed she was put in the same group as me. I breathed a sigh of relief knowing I wouldn't be alone.

They placed the three of us on the third floor of some old dorm and we discovered it had no air conditioning. Ugh! The twins were at the end of the corridor and I was two doors down. After unpacking I hurried to their room. Since they slept practically the whole way, I was looking forward to catching up on the latest – their two-day trip to New York City.

Their mother had finally given in to Tori's pleading and allowed her to do some modeling there. I wanted all the details. Tori said it was mostly for catalogs, like sports clothes and stuff. She was hoping her agency could get her hooked up with companies like Nike or Champion. I went on high alert, and asked her if she thought they might give away free stuff, but she didn't think so.

I wondered why Jules didn't do this modeling stuff, too, since she and Tori looked pretty much alike. But Jules said she hated having her picture taken and could never stand still that long.

I totally got the standing still part. If it was me, I'd be all over the place. They'd probably have to use a video camera to get one picture. I asked Tori if anyone showed models eating Italian food 'cause I was pretty sure I could slow down for a dish of pasta and marinara sauce.

She laughed and said I couldn't hold a forkful of food midway between my mouth and the plate long enough for the photographer to snap a single picture. I told her she was being mean and she said, "No, just honest."

I heard a knock on the door. It was one of my favorite teammates, Heather Whitcraft. Around school she seemed more like the cheerleader type, all bubbly blond, with her aren't-I-cool clothes and perfect nails, but once the whistle blew, forget about it. She played as hard and determined as anyone. Seeing Heather, it hit me that most of our team from last year would soon be together. I was psyched.

When Heather mentioned who she was sharing a room with, it got me wondering who I would be staying with. A month ago it was all set and then my friend, Ellen Burns, hurt her knee and had to have surgery.

"What if they stick you with a stranger?" Tori asked.

"They wouldn't do that, would they?" I asked.

Tori shrugged her shoulders. Her question made me jumpy. I didn't want to have to buddy-up with someone from another school, and spending any one-on-one time with one of Northfield's upperclassmen would be even worse.

Another knock broke up my worry moment and before long the room felt like it had shrunk to the size of a closet. Most of my classmates must have figured that this was the place to be and the room began to buzz with the steady hum of all the tales of summer vacation. Every once in a while I could hear a "no way" or "she didn't" which probably meant the story was an especially juicy one.

Someone suggested we make this the official sophomore meeting room, but Tori made it conditional. "Meetings can only be scheduled in the P.M.," she said.

"That's right you guys, our first order of business is to make sure Tori gets to the fields on time each morning," Jules said.

Tori threw a pillow at Jules. "I'm not that bad," she said.

"Yes, you are," Jules and I said in unison.

Jules looked at her watch. "Hey, we better get our stuff together. We have to report to the main field at three o'clock."

My pulse leaped. It was all starting.

*　　*　　*

I went to my room and found another one of my class-mates, Lindsay Sayers, unpacking.

"Hey, Linds, I'm sure glad it's you."

"They didn't tell you?" she asked as she shut a drawer and turned around to face me.

"No. I had no idea 'til I just walked in."

Lindsay finished her unpacking by turning her suitcase upside down, and dumping whatever was left into the bottom drawer. "You okay with it?" she asked.

"Sure, why wouldn't I be?"

"I don't know. Skip it," she said as she stored her suitcase under the bed.

I was searching for something else to say when I heard the sound of cleats moving past our room. *Here we go.* I could feel my pulse accelerate, and quickly grabbed my gear.

As we made our way down the dorm steps toward the main field, we were joined by all the other Northfield players. It seemed to me like freshman year all over again, athletes slyly checking each other out. Only this time it was our class and the upperclassmen who were doing the once-overs with each other.

Jules looked around to make sure everyone was accounted for. Sometimes she was like a mother hen checking on her chicks. Other times she was our field commander. I didn't know what we would do without her. Most players were usually happy to have her in charge, although sometimes I would hear grumbling.

Two of the starters from last year's freshman team were not in camp – Caitlin Grant and Sam Jones. Someone asked why Caitlin didn't come.

"She's still on vacation with her family," Heather said. "She hoped she wouldn't have to go. Her father told her that family came first, so camp was out."

"That kind of stinks," Lindsay said.

"I know," Heather went on, "Caitlin cried for days, but her father wouldn't budge. I told her we would help her catch up when practice starts."

"I still think it's lousy," Lindsay said. "She's old enough not to go on family vacations. I'm lucky my mom gets how important sports are to me."

"Yeah, Lindsay, but be fair. You and your mom can plan things together, and as long as she can get off work, you don't have to worry about anybody else," Jules said.

Lindsay gave Jules the evil eye. What Jules said was true, but she shouldn't have said it like she did. Sometimes Jules stormed through things when it came to Lindsay and forgot Lindsay was kind of sensitive about not having a dad and being an only child. The two of them worked fine on the field, but maybe not so much off it.

I tried to take a little of the heat out of the air and changed the subject. "What about Sam?"

"I was hoping she would be able to make it," Anna Merlino said. "It would be so good for her."

I wondered if Sam and her family couldn't afford camp, which would be a shame 'cause Sam loved hockey. And even though we weren't rich and my mom wasn't keen on me going to a sports camp, she hadn't put her foot down and said no, at least not this time.

*       *       *

At the field we found ourselves surrounded by a bazillion hockey players. I'd never seen so many athletes in one place. Nerves bubbled up on my skin as I waited for things to start, and for a moment I wished I was back in freshman year and didn't know how many players there were in the world.

As we watched more girls filing onto the field, Heather gave us the low-down about camp, stuff she had learned from her older sister. "Our groups are only temporary," she said. "The coaches are going to evaluate us in our first session, and then we'll be put in permanent groups."

I thought this was a stupid idea. I didn't need to be evaluated. I just wanted to play with my friends. Suddenly camp didn't seem like such a fun place to be. I started chewing on my lower lip and gripped my stick a little tighter.

After the camp director welcomed us, we were sent off to our assigned fields. I was sure glad to have Tori by my side. Our coach for the afternoon, who was a senior at the university, took us through stick work drills for half an hour then had us play some 7v7.

It was really different playing with girls from other schools. I couldn't figure out when to make my move, and didn't know what players wanted me to do when they didn't open their mouths and talk. A lot of the girls in the group played blast ball, just hitting the ball hard and having me chase it. It was **so** not how Northfield played.

Afterwards, the coach told us to check the camp bulletin board after dinner to learn what groups we would be in for the rest of camp. She said the nighttime would be for team play. I sure hoped that meant all us sophomores would be a team and not mixed in with the upperclassmen.

# - 3 -

At dinner, my friends and I staked out our unofficial place at camp, claiming two tables at the far end of the dining hall. Midway through the meal, Tori pointed to a group of girls sitting on the other side of the room.

"Hey, there're the upperclassmen," she said.

A memory flashed in my mind of another cafeteria, freshman year. That's where my buddies from eighth grade first encountered our old rivals, the girls from Morristown Middle School. It had taken a long time for all of us freshmen to get together and become one team. I wondered if it would be the same thing all over again this year with the upperclassmen. I glanced at Jules. She was staring across the cafeteria with a steely expression on her face. Lindsay caught my eye, and I knew she was silently thinking about last year, too.

Two coaches came into the cafeteria and tacked a bunch of lists to the camp bulletin board. Lindsay and I hurried over with Jules and Heather not far behind. I scanned down the alphabetical list of campers. I found my name and saw the group I was assigned to. Then I quickly ran my finger back up the list to check for the twins and felt myself relax. I wasn't going to be alone during the day. Jules and I had been assigned to the same group. Tori, Lindsay, and Heather would be together in a different group.

We were listed by high school teams for the evening competition. Northfield had twice as many players as any other school, so we were divided into two teams, Northfield 1 and Northfield 2, with all of us sophomores being together in Northfield 2.

We read the evening tournament rules. Each team was assigned to one of two divisions, East or West. Northfield 1 was in the East and our team was in the West. We would have two games each evening and would get two points for a win and one point for a tie. The top team in the East division would play the top West division team for the camp championship on Saturday morning, the last day of camp. It looked like great fun and the four of us were getting pumped just reading about it.

We went back to the table and gave the others the low-down. Then I got to thinking. *It was a long shot, but suppose, just suppose both Northfield teams won their divisions.* I shook my head at the idea. That would be way too much drama.

\*     \*     \*

That night our first opponent was another New Jersey team. While we were waiting to go on the field, our goalies, Becky and Kerry, gave us a heads-up they were mighty tired from their workouts that afternoon.

"What are you talking about?" Lindsay asked. "You guys don't even do any running."

"Maybe not as much as you," Becky said, "but we'll challenge you to lunges and squats anytime."

Anna put her arm around Becky's shoulders and said, "Don't worry. Your defense can handle things if you're not tough enough."

That got Becky going and pretty soon it was a smackdown between the goalies and the rest of us, but it was all in fun. I mean, I couldn't ever imagine how hard it is to be a goalie and have balls flying at you and I think the rest of the team felt the same.

It took us a little while to realize that there were three other players standing close by who were wearing the same color scrimmage vests as us. Tori, always the outgoing one, walked over to one of the strangers and asked the girl her name.

The girl said, sarcastically, "Leftover." Her answer froze Tori in mid-stride and the girl laughed. "Just kidding, I'm Gabby, and this is Jess and Molly. We're juniors." Curious as to what was going on, Anna and I listened in as the girl continued. "We thought we'd be with the others, but some of the seniors kind of pushed us to come with you guys," she said.

Molly interrupted, "They think we're not as good as them, but I don't see much difference in any of us juniors, except maybe Kate Carson. She played some varsity last year."

"Well, we're glad you're here. We were worried we would have to play short. It'll be fun, you'll see," said Tori.

The juniors glanced at each other. Then Jess said, "We weren't sure how you all would take having to play with us. It's been awhile since last year and we didn't know if you'd be too happy to see us. Besides, you guys are so tight."

Anna and I looked at each other, surprised by what the girl said. "What do you mean we're so ..." Anna said. She never had a chance to finish her thought, though, as the ref blew her whistle for us to come onto the field.

I was surprised to discover that the juniors weren't really any better than any of us sophomores, and one, I thought, was way weaker. Still, we won the game easily enough, 3-0.

"Hey thanks," Gabby said after the game. "That was fun. You guys *are* really good."

As we all were walking away from the field, Jess turned to me and said, "You know some of us were really sorry about last year. Not everyone wanted to haze you guys. Your team handled it with a lot of class. I was really embarrassed afterwards."

I smiled and wondered how many other upperclassmen felt like Jess.

\*     \*     \*

Later that night, as we were getting ready for bed, I told Lindsay what Jess had said.

"They should feel that way," said Lindsay. "That was a scary night."

Both of us remembered the cold October night last year when the upperclassmen took us freshmen to the middle of the woods and had us dance, blindfolded, in front of a bunch of guys and be totally humiliated.

"The whole thing was ridiculous," Lindsay said. "It would never have happened if the JV hadn't been such babies, whining to the seniors just because we beat them in that scrimmage."

"Yeah, but that was no excuse. The seniors didn't have to listen to them. I hated that night. We're never going to do that to the new freshmen," I said.

"You're right about that," Lindsay said, turning over in her bed. "Night, Jackie."

"Hey, Linds," I said, and she rolled back to face me. "I meant to tell you, you look great. Have you lost weight or something?"

Lindsay smiled into the dark, "No, I just grew two more inches, plus Mother Nature finally caught up with me. For awhile there, I thought it was never going to happen. Thanks for noticing. Night, Jack," she said, and turned over and quickly fell asleep.

It amazed me how different we all were, even though we were the same age. Lindsay was the last of us, I guessed, to go through that crazy awkward phase. You know, when your body isn't exactly little girl, but not grownup either. When we were younger, guys called her 'woodchuck' 'cause of her teeth and the way she was built, which was really crummy. I looked over at her now, remembering how she looked on the field tonight. Her braces were off and she wasn't chunky anymore, that was for sure.

As I drifted off to sleep, I was thinking about one of those old TV shows where they bring out people that used to know you back when, and then you turn out to be this 'hottie,' and now they're jealous and sorry they called you names. That would be so cool for Lindsay. I thought she would definitely have the last laugh on a lot of people. I'd really like to be around to see that one.

\*     \*     \*

After breakfast the next morning, Jules and I said good-bye to the other girls and headed out to our field. We soon discovered there were two other Northfield players in our group – a girl named Mandy Stevenson, and Kate Carson, the junior that Molly had mentioned. Our coach turned out to be a college coach and she asked us to call her Sue. She told us that we were one of the top groups in camp so she expected a lot from us.

*Yikes!*

I looked at Jules. "What are we doing here?" I whispered.

Jules, who must have been at least five foot ten by then, looked down at me, "Relax, we're just about to get our money's worth."

"What do you mean?"

"We're going to pick up some really good stuff being in this group. It'll be great, you'll see," she said.

It was easy for Jules to think like that 'cause she loved a challenge – me, I was a little nervous that I might be in over my head.

And it sure felt that way as the session started. The coach went through the drills – bing, bang, boom. The pace was nothing like freshman hockey. Last year our coach worked us hard, but we had a lot of fun joking around, too. No one was goofing around here. Everyone seemed focused, standing in line, anxiously waiting their turn.

It was going way too fast and I began tripping all over myself. I just wanted to shrink and disappear. Surprisingly, Sue didn't yell, call me stupid, or send me to some beginner group. It helped that Jules was my partner. She was such a steady, dependable player, and eventually I started to calm down and got into the flow. Toward the end of the session the other two Northfield girls asked us to switch with them and I started partnering with this Mandy Stevenson.

We'd gone through a couple of drills when Mandy elbowed me and said playfully, "Chill! You're doing fine." Then she grinned and said, "I think Northfield might have another McKendry star on the horizon."

I smiled at her reference to my soccer-playing brother, Matt, who had just graduated from Northfield. To be honest, what Mandy said did make me feel better, especially when I found out she was a senior.

At the end of the morning session, the four of us walked off the field together and we started talking about the upcoming season. "We lost most of the varsity team to graduation so we're in for a major rebuilding this season," Mandy said. "We know your class has potential, but some of the juniors and seniors have waited a long time to have their shot at varsity. They're going to really fight for those positions, so look out."

Kate chimed in, "They won't be happy if any of you sophomores try to take what they think is rightfully theirs. Not to scare you or anything, but we're just giving you both a heads-up."

"How do you two feel about sophomores playing varsity?" Jules asked as we climbed the steps to the cafeteria.

Mandy gave Kate a look. Then Kate said, "We don't care. We just want to win."

I saw Jules kind of chewing on that one, and then she nodded and said, "Fair enough."

I just listened to the whole thing. I was kind of surprised that Mandy and Kate were so nice and so up front with us, too, with the competition thing. Anyway I didn't have any worries on that score since I was expecting to spend all my time on JV.

*      *      *

We left Mandy and Kate to search out the other sopho-mores and found everyone had stories to tell. Anna loved her coach who worked at a local high school. As Anna was going on about how much fun she had, I was thinking that fun was definitely not one of the words that I would have used to describe my morning. More like scary, stressful, and yeah, exciting, too.

Tori was busy examining an apple, turning it round and round looking for the perfect spot for her first bite. She must have found it 'cause her hands became still and she said, "Jules, what's your group like?"

I stopped my grazing and waited to see what Jules would say. This could be tricky 'cause I was sure Jules didn't want Tori to feel bad if she discovered that her group wasn't as strong as ours was.

"It's a good group, Jules answered carefully. "Everybody works hard. It's mostly players from Pennsylvania, but there are two Northfield upperclassmen. Do you have any in your group, Tori?"

*Jules, you are a smooth one.* I wondered how a person our age learned to think so fast like that. I could tell that Tori bought into Jules' answer and was relieved the moment passed with no one feeling like they were better or worse than anyone else.

"Hey, you guys," Heather said. "You won't believe it, but our coach is a guy. "Can you imagine it? A male field hockey player!"

"Field hockey is a big sport world-wide for men, only soccer is more popular. I think it's just getting going for guys here in the States," Anna said.

We looked at her, like, what?

"I read it in a book somewhere," she said sounding a little embarrassed like we caught her out reading non-essentials, like extra credit or something.

There was a moment at the table while we all kind of digested what Anna said about field hockey all over the world, and then knowing how boy-crazy Tori was I asked, "So, Tori … is he hot enough for you?"

Tori stuck her tongue out at me, and I grinned, shaking my head and saying, "Tori, there's one guy in this whole camp and you manage to land him. You're amazing." That left everyone at the table laughing, except Tori of course, who pretended to pout.

\*     \*     \*

The days at camp passed quickly. Jules and I were getting a ton better 'cause we were surrounded by such good players. Walking off the field one morning, Jules said to me, "Some of these girls are so easy to play with."

"Yeah, like everything they do kind of makes sense, but sometimes …" my voice trailed off and I shook my head. "Sometimes the ball moves too quickly," I said.

Jules stopped to take off her cleats and slip into her flip-flops. "I know what you mean," she said. "Defense is so much faster, too. If I blink, I'm done."

"Do you think we'll finally catch on?"

"The next three years will be awfully long if we can't," Jules said, laughing. She threw her shoes over her shoulder and started to walk away in her usual purposeful way.

Hurrying to catch up, I couldn't understand how Jules could always be so confident while I was bouncing around, one moment feeling like I had it all under control, and then another, believing I was the worst hockey player that ever existed.

# - 4 -

After Wednesday night's games, there was a knock on the door. It was Mandy Stevenson. "The other seniors and I have decided to have a team get-together, nine o'clock in the dorm's rec room," she said. "I'll tell the juniors, and you guys let all the other sophs know. Okay?"

All I could think of was – another hazing! It must have shown on my face 'cause Mandy's mouth kind of tightened, and she said, "Don't worry, it's nothing bad."

After she left, I turned to Lindsay who was busy putting a new grip on her stick. "For a moment there I thought it was going to be déjà vu all over again," I said.

Lindsay looked up from her work, grinning, "That'll never happen. We're a whole lot tougher than we were a year ago."

I hoped Lindsay was right, but even if we were tougher, that didn't mean much if the older girls didn't like us.

\*     \*     \*

There was a sign on the door – Northfield Team Meeting. The word 'team' seemed kind of funny to me. Did the older girls really believe we were one?

Once we settled in, Mandy stood up, introduced herself to everyone as the team captain, and welcomed us all to camp.

*Wow, the captain and she's so nice.* I watched her take a deep breath like someone facing a crucial challenge.

"I was going to postpone what I'm going to say," she said, "but I don't think it can wait."

I could sense a little nervousness running through the room. Mandy must have felt it, too, but she plunged ahead.

"I know the last time we were all together wasn't such a fun time for everyone. I think we need to put last year behind us. If we don't, I'm not sure what kind of a season we'll have this year."

I didn't know either. We seemed like a bunch of jigsaw pieces scattered around the room. Was a captain's job to put all the pieces together? I thought it would take everyone. I didn't envy Mandy one bit.

Mandy went on. "Since the coaches don't know what went on last year, I think it would be better to get everything off our chests here at camp. Then, maybe we can move forward. What do you think?"

I thought about how freezing cold and scary it was out in the woods, and how obnoxious the upperclassmen and their friends were to us. Worse, they had left us alone there in the dark, all tied up together. We couldn't even get the blindfolds off. Luckily someone had a penknife, and we were able to eventually free ourselves and find our way out of the woods. Otherwise, we would have been out there all night.

We wound up on some country road, and had to hitch a ride with a trucker who helped us get to my house where we had a big sleepover. The one good thing that happened was that when we woke the next morning, we had finally become a team.

We never told anyone what happened. It was a deal we made with the upperclassmen. My parents suspected something weird had gone on, but they thought it was all in good fun, and not the nasty thing it really was. After it was all over, we knew we'd been lucky 'cause so much could have gone wrong that night. It could have been a disaster.

I glanced around the room and wondered what everybody was thinking. No one was making eye contact. Girls were just busy staring at the floor, or their fingernails, or something. I looked up. Mandy was standing perfectly still. It was like she was paralyzed and wouldn't be able to move until somebody said something.

I knew she was trying to do the right thing. The meeting was important for all of us. But I didn't see any fairy godmother in the room that could cast a magic spell and make the past go 'poof' and disappear.

The silence in the room seemed to go on and on. It made me feel itchy like something needed to happen. I usually would never speak up, except with my friends, but I could feel words creeping to the front of my mouth, wanting to escape.

"I don't think last year's get-together or whatever you call it should ever happen again," I said, finally. My voice sounded shaky and weak, like a little mouse, even to my own ears. Embarrassed, I decided to clam up. Then I started thinking about that night, and kept on going. "It could have gotten very dangerous if you think about it," I said. "Someone could have gotten sick from the cold. We could have gotten hit by a car trying to find our way home. Some creep could have come along ..."

I was interrupted by a girl I didn't know. "Look, it just got out of hand. Not everyone was thinking."

I lowered my eyes, and could feel heat coming to my face. It was like the girl didn't want to hear just how bad a night it really was. But my courage had run its course, and I bit my tongue.

A small, stocky girl next to Mandy stood up. "Hi, I'm Beth Walton, senior goalie. Before we go any further why doesn't everybody say their name so we can get to know each other?"

While we went around the room, I watched Mandy. I could tell by the way she leaned back on the arm of the sofa and crossed her arms that she was kind of glad to move in another direction for a minute.

After the introductions, another girl spoke up. It was Bri, the girl from the rest stop. "It's great you're all here, of course," she said, "but I don't think that last year was such a big deal."

There was some grumbling, but Bri ignored it, and continued. "I will say it probably shouldn't be repeated because we don't want to break school rules against hazing. That'll only get us in a whole lot of trouble if we're caught."

When Tori asked the upperclassmen why they did it, one of the juniors said, "The coaches were always talking about you guys all the time, how good you were going to be and stuff. It was getting on our nerves."

A senior, I think she said her name was Kat, pretty much said the same thing. Then she said, "When you guys scrimmaged us, you got all intense, and showed us up in front of our coach. Some people thought you needed to be put in your place. I guess you could say the hazing was a payback."

"Maybe the coaches' talking was to get you guys fired up," Anna said.

I caught a couple of the seniors whispering to each other, not really listening to what Anna was saying. It got me riled again, but sticking my neck out once was enough.

Then Heather said the perfect thing. "You guys need to know, most of us like playing hard. It's just a fact. My sister used to play varsity at Northfield, and she told me if we wanted to be good we would have to push each other. Do you guys think she was wrong?"

I saw some upperclassmen kind of shake their heads like they agreed with Heather. Others were hard to read. I figured some of the older girls felt that last year had been a big mistake, but not everyone. I started chewing on my nails, and got the feeling that things weren't settled by a long shot.

"Well," Mandy said, "does anyone else have anything to add?" Since no one spoke up she said, "Okay, I guess everyone is tired and probably just a little bit sore."

Now that was something we all could agree on since everyone was groaning. Then Mandy suggested that tomorrow night we all try to get to each other's night games if we could. She ended the meeting by having us all come together for a Northfield cheer and everyone started to squeeze together in the small space. To an outsider we might have looked like a typical team, but it seemed more like a fourth grade gym class to me. One where the boys thought if they got too close to a girl they would get cooties or something.

As we climbed the stairs, they seemed like a mountain, with my quads tight from all the sprinting. My legs definitely needed to be stretched. I was thinking the season ahead looked a little bit like a mountain, too, and wished peoples' minds could be stretched as easily as muscles.

Lindsay caught up to me on the second landing. "That was gutsy in there, calling them on what they did. I don't think I could have spoken up like that."

"I wasn't planning on it Linds, but no one was saying anything. I felt bad for Mandy standing there with everyone just kind of letting her hang. And, she was right. We needed to get things out in the open and move on."

"She was trying, I'll give her that," Lindsay said.

The meeting reminded me that there was a heck of a lot more to sports than running through a bunch of drills. The season ahead sure looked like it might be filled with some mighty deep potholes.

*     *     *

Later, as we were getting ready for bed, there was a knock on the door. "Guys, you up?" The door opened. It was Jules. "Do you have a minute?" she asked

"Sure, come and sit down," I said, and slid over on the bed to make room for her.

"Thanks for saying something tonight, Jackie. I guess you wondered why I stayed quiet since I'm usually the one who always has something to say." She gave a little smile, and then glanced at Lindsay. "I know it gets old sometimes."

Lindsay stared at some spot on the wall, like she was counting the cracks in the plaster or something.

Jules ignored Lindsay's silence and went on. "Tonight I was glad you and the others spoke up instead of me. I'm still so angry about last year. Whatever I would have said would have never come out right."

I was surprised that Jules still felt so strongly about last year. Usually she was able to let the past go and concentrate on what was right in front of her. It was one of the things that made her such a good leader. She was right about one thing, though. It probably wasn't fair for the rest of us to expect her to always be the one who did all the talking. I just hoped she wasn't counting on me.

"Wow, Miss Perfect finally let her hair down," Lindsay said when we were finally alone. "It makes me feel like she is almost normal, like the rest of us mortals."

"Lindsay," I said, "that's a lousy thing to say."

"Well, it's true. Everybody thinks she's so great, and here's proof that she doesn't have the answers either. Just like the rest of us."

I pulled my sheet around me, and started to think about what Jules had said. It was always so easy to let Jules or Tori take charge, thinking that they just liked doing it. And, even if they did, people could still complain, and Lindsay was number one on the complaining list. It seemed like being a leader was a no-win situation for sure. 'Becoming a team' stuff was way too complicated, and I wondered why we couldn't all just go out and play.

# - 5 -

I dreaded Thursday's practice. We were going to be working on skills I couldn't do – for the entire session, too! At least when a coach was making you do something hard, she should be breaking it up with something you're good at, was my way thinking. Then, at least your ego wouldn't be stuck in that 'you're just pathetic' mode for the whole practice.

The session started with me feeling kind of grumpy, dragging my feet, since I knew one thing that was coming – the dreaded lifting the ball in the air. I'd never been able to get the hang of it no matter how hard I tired. As I stared at the offending ball, I thought about gluing a bunch of Mexican jumping beans all over it, and then maybe it would have no choice, but to go airborne.

Then, Sue showed us by just changing our grip our stick would act like a ramp, and the ball could be forced off the ground. After a couple of tries, I started to get it. Magic! All of a sudden I was this happy goofball, jogging all over the field, making the ball do little flips off the ground. Sometimes the simplest things made me happy.

Sue must have seen my excitement. I don't think anyone could have missed it. She walked over to me and said, "Solving a problem doesn't always have to be some big mysterious mountain to climb. Sometimes it just takes one little thing. But you do have to keep at it 'til you discover it."

I kind of liked what she said, and figured it was one of those important ideas that I needed to tuck in the back of my mind, ready to be pulled out at some 'I can't do it' moment in the future.

When it came to practicing the 1v1's, I felt way more challenged. I'd always counted on my speed to get by, but camp had taught me that being fast wasn't enough. Sue told us how fakes could get defenders to do one thing, and then you could do something else. After she demonstrated a couple of fakes, a light bulb went on in my head, and I got it. I was pumped.

The day suddenly turned all sunshiny, and I wondered what it might be like to be a coach like Sue someday. But then I'd have to teach, too, and stand up in front of a class with everybody staring at me. I pondered that picture for a minute, and then my little coaching fantasy wisely disappeared.

*     *     *

That night our team was playing our toughest opponent yet. We had heard through the camp rumor mill that the team had been New York State semi-finalists the year before. Everyone in camp figured that they would take our division.

Molly told us that their big gun was the center forward, and in the warmup we picked her out right away. She was banging balls into the cage, sending us a message – like, forget about it.

In our pre-game huddle, I turned to Jules. "What are we going to do?"

"She can't score if she doesn't have the ball," she said.

So that was it. We decided if our attack blocked the passing lanes to her and we had one of our defender's mark her tight we'd be alright. Jess volunteered to play her, saying she was used to speedy players after playing against Northfield's varsity all last year.

As the half started, both teams were kind of tentative, feeling each other out. The two defenses were talking up a storm, so it was hard for the attackers to get the ball moving anywhere. With less than a minute to play in the half, our defense got caught up in the speed of play and stopped communicating.

The New York team sent a long pass down the middle of the field to their star, and she took off. Jules was the only defender left to stop her. As good as she was, Jules was no match for this player. The girl slipped past her in one quick move and slammed the ball into the cage. Ten seconds later the whistle blew for the half.

At the halftime break, Tori asked, "What are we going to do? We're so busy worrying about that girl we've had no opportunities to score."

I was downing water as fast as I could and handed the bottle to the person next to me. "We're thinking about her too much," I said. "We haven't even had a shot on goal."

"Your right," Jules said. "We need to do something else."

We finally decided that Jess would just have to front the girl, and then the rest of us would have to play more aggressively and take more chances. So we had a new plan. We just didn't know if it was going to work.

As I turned to go back out on the field I noticed six or seven upperclassmen watching us. I didn't know if their being there was a show of support or if they were simply checking us out, but I figured that focusing on the New York team was probably more important.

Jess kept the girl away from the ball, and as the second half moved along Heather and Tori became more confident and began going after more loose balls.

With a minute left, Heather intercepted a ball just inside our attacking twenty-five. She hit the ball toward the striking circle, and I sprinted after it. Out came the New York goalkeeper, and she slid along the ground and blocked my shot. But she couldn't clear it away and the ball sat right in front of her outstretched body. I knew I couldn't hit it into her. That'd be a foul. So without really thinking I shifted my hands on my stick, just like Sue showed me, and lifted the ball over the goalkeeper and her outstretched hands. The ball rolled into the empty cage.

I turned away from the cage and saw my teammates running up to me. I was grinning from ear to ear.

"Jackie, way to go"

"Great job!"

"We did it, awesome!"

The comments flew around me as we ran back to the center of the field to restart play. Thirty seconds later the final whistle blew.

"What happens now?" one of us asked the referee.

"The next game has to start in five minutes," the referee said. "Don't worry. Your team will get credit for the tie, but who plays for the championship depends on how everyone does in tomorrow's games."

We all crowded around one another, so excited that we pulled off the tie. "Jess, you did great," Jules said.

Jess smiled, "It felt good and ..."

Something caught Jess's eye and left her speechless. We turned in the direction she was staring. Someone was walking toward us. Someone we didn't expect to see. It was Mrs. Fortunato, Northfield's varsity coach. She was a legend. Because of her, Northfield field hockey was known throughout the state, and a ton of conference championship plaques and three state championship trophies were sitting in our school's display case. She had been my gym teacher freshman year, and boy, was she tough and no-nonsense.

Suddenly it got quiet, our excitement in a holding pattern. This was our new coach. We held our breath wondering if she saw the game, and if we did okay in front of her. Despite the whistles in the background, and the sound of the next game going on, all we noticed was her, getting closer and closer.

Her face gave us no hint of what she was thinking. When she reached us she said, "So girls, what about that game?"

No one said boo. I mean, who wanted to single themselves out in front of one of the top coaches in the state and say something stupid? None of us, not even Jules. Mrs. Fortunato was waiting for an answer. Something inside me screamed, *say something.*

"We think we did pretty well," I said, trying to keep my voice light, as if she and I had casual conversations like this all the time.

"Why's that, Jackie? It was a tie."

By now the others were **so** glad they didn't speak up 'cause it was me on the hot seat now, and not them. I could feel the tightness in my chest. *What's the matter with me opening my big mouth?* My brain started to shut down, so I quickly said the first thing that came to my mind.

"Because we figured out how to stop them," I said. "We had a game plan and it worked."

She stared directly at me, kind of eyeball to eyeball, and then a smile broke out on her face. She looked around at the rest of our team standing there and said, "Yes, and it was an excellent one, too. Congratulations! It was very exciting to see you work together. And, Jess," she said, "I **will** remember the job you did on that center forward. I'm going to go watch some other hockey now, but I'll see you girls soon."

Jess was beaming after Mrs. Fortunato left, and Becky slapped me on the back. "Way to go, Jackie."

"Come on," Molly said. "We'd better go cheer for the others." As we walked over to the field where the older girls were playing, and my heart rate started getting back to normal, I wondered if Mrs. Fortunato would be as happy with the upperclassmen as she was with us. I sure hoped so for everyone's sake.

\*     \*     \*

On Friday, our team still hadn't lost, so after our evening game we waited around the camp bulletin board to check on the scores as they were posted. The main thing we were looking for was how the New York team would do in their final game. When one of the coaches put up the final scores it was unbelievable – New York had tied again. That meant we were playing for the camp championship.

Our upperclassmen were not so lucky in their division. They had been in a tie for first place with a team from Virginia, and then the camp director broke the tie saying that the team with the most goals would move on and play for the championship. It turned out to be the Virginia team.

The upperclassmen were totally bummed. Lindsay heard one of them say that we were just lucky, that we had the easier division. Maybe that was true, but I was glad we weren't playing our older girls. If we had faced each other I think it would have been like broken mirrors, walking under ladders, and having a black cat walk across our path, all rolled up into one.

* * *

After breakfast the next morning, I walked over to the tray-return counter. Bri and Allison were already there waiting in line to stack their trays. I overheard Bri say, "I'm sick of those sophomores. Everything is always going their way. None of them better have any ideas about playing varsity."

Allison gave Bri a nudge. Bri looked over her shoulder at me and realized I must have overheard her. She looked annoyed that she was caught out. But, maybe it was me, and I just annoyed her in general. It was kind of hard to tell.

"I don't care," she said looking back to Allison. Then she turned to me. "Last year is done. You sophomores need to get over yourselves. Got it?"

I blinked. I couldn't thing of a thing to say, and I felt myself grow cold inside. The two of them waited for a reaction, and finding none, they turned, threw their trays on the counter, and walked away. I stood there, and for a moment I just wanted to be home. Not play hockey. Just be a normal 'go to school and come home at three o'clock' kind of girl.

* * *

Warming up for the championship game, I was kind of on automatic pilot, still mulling over what happened at breakfast, when Anna asked, "Do you think they'll come and cheer for us?"

"No way. They're still pouting," Lindsay said, as she pushed the ball to me.

"Some of them might," I said hopefully, thinking of Kate and Mandy.

Within the first fifteen minutes of the game the score was unfortunately 0-2, them, and we knew we were in trouble. The Virginia team was way smarter than us, and their stick skills were awesome.

As the game went on, Bri's comments faded as quickly as any chances of us winning. They managed to hold us scoreless and slipped another one in against us just before the final whistle blew. Standing together with my teammates afterwards, giving the winners a cheer, I thought that as long as my friends were with me on the field, players like Bri might not matter so much. Maybe I could ignore the older girls altogether. I looked over at the sidelines. I didn't see a single upperclassman.

## - 6 -

When Mom and Dad picked us up, three very tired hockey players stumbled into the car. I thought we could sleep for a week.

"Did you have fun, honey?" Mom asked.

"It was great. The coaches were so cool."

"That's nice," she said.

I noticed her eyes had that glazed-over look, though, which meant she didn't really care all that much about camp. She was just pretending to show interest 'cause that's what moms were supposed to do.

Dad said, "We have a little surprise for you when we get home."

"What? What is it, Dad?"

"Oh, you'll have to wait," he laughed.

I thought about home and my brother and sister. Being away at camp had kind of made me forget that the rest of the world even existed. Sort of like time traveling, except the date stayed the same.

All that thinking must have made my brain a little tired. Soon I was fast asleep. I must have been more exhausted than

I thought 'cause I didn't wake until I felt the car slow down. We were at the twins' house.

Once we left them off, and I was almost home, I was on high alert. Dad looked at me in the rearview mirror and said, "So how much do you love your brother?"

"Tons, Dad, why?"

"You'll see," he answered mysteriously.

When we pulled into the drive and got to the front door, my brother, Matt, was waiting with a big grin on his face. He was wearing his old soccer shorts and a T-shirt turned inside out, and he was covered in paint from head to toe.

"What's going on?" I asked, laughing at the sight of him, yet puzzled, too.

"Come on, I'll show you," he said.

He jogged upstairs, down the hall, and into his bedroom, with me right on his heels. The walls of the room were no longer beige, but a color that was somewhere between a pale orange and peach. It was just the shade I had found in a magazine and had pointed out to my mom.

When my parents had first told me I could have Matt's old room once he went away to college, I had felt a twinge of guilt, but he had laughed and said, "Don't worry, Dad promised to build me a cool place down in the basement."

I looked around the freshly painted room now. Matt was watching me. He waved his finger at me. "Don't get any ideas, the room's still mine until I leave for school," he said.

The rest of the family came to the doorway, and Mom said, "We thought we'd leave everything like it is, and buy you a new bedspread and curtains. Then you can put whatever you want on the walls."

My little sister Lizzie snuck around Mom and said, "Now I can have a room, just for me. But I'm keeping the twin beds so I can have sleepovers."

When Dad pointed out that no one was mentioning sleepovers for eight-year-olds, Lizzie stamped off, saying, "No fair! Everyone has fun but me."

Laughing and shaking his head at Lizzie's comment, Matt said, "Look out Dad, Jackie and I are a piece of cake compared to the time you're going to have with mighty mite there."

Then Matt turned on his big brother face and said, "Now that you've gotten a week of rest lounging around at that hockey camp of yours, it's time to help me get my new room ready. We've got the dry wall up now, so we have to tape and spackle."

I made a face at his 'lounging around' comment. Matt grinned and said, "But seriously, "Happy Birthday, Jackie."

It was then I realized that tomorrow was going to be my birthday. Being away at camp had made me completely forget about the date. I was finally going to be fifteen and would be getting the one thing I had wanted for so long, well, besides the room, and that was my own cell phone. I was psyched. I couldn't imagine anything topping this.

*       *       *

The next morning I woke to find my little sister nestled up against my back. "Hey, what's up squirt?" I asked, as I turned around to face her.

"I wanted to be the first one to wish you a happy birthday."

"Thanks, Lizzie," I said, as I reached out to rearrange her bangs, and wondered why she was the lucky one to have our mom's golden blond hair while I was stuck with my fiery red curls.

There was a time, when I was younger, that I thought I must have been adopted 'cause I seemed to be the only redhead in the family. Then one day Grandma McKendry showed me a picture of her husband, the grandfather I never knew, and sure enough, his hair was the same as mine, and that was that. I was definitely a McKendry.

Lizzie started to pout 'cause I wasn't giving her my full attention. She pushed out her lower lip and said, "I'm going to miss you."

"Oh, Lizzie, you're going to love having your own room. You can decorate it anyway you want and I won't be waking you up in the morning getting ready for school." That seemed to make her feel better 'cause she gave me a quick hug, then bounced off the bed and went downstairs.

My fifteenth birthday flew by, and by the end of the day I was busy uploading my friends' phone numbers to my new cell phone. *The first call I make will be to the twins.* I wished I could text, but my parents didn't put it on the plan. They said it was too distracting. I decided that when I grew up I'd let my kids have a cell phone the moment they hit kindergarten.

Just then the house phone rang. Mom called up from the kitchen, "Jackie, for you."

"Hello," I said into the phone, wondering who it could be. A male voice started singing, "Happy, Happy Birthday, Baby." A big smile spread across my face.

"Mitch, I can't believe you remembered," I said, when the singing ended.

"Reds, what kind of boyfriend would I be if I forgot? How was your birthday?"

I gave him every detail and then told him about camp.

After we hung up, I was about bouncing off my bed with excitement 'cause he'd told me he'd be flying in Sunday and hoped to see me the next day. I couldn't wait.

*    *    *

The week following camp was definitely payback time for getting my own room. By Thursday Matt's room was ready for paint. "What color you picking, Matt?" I asked, as we sat eating breakfast.

"I need to put a primer coat on first, and then we'll use masking tape to block off an area near the ceiling for some stripes that'll go all the way around the room. We'll paint the rest of the room tan, and then tomorrow we'll paint the stripes in my school colors – one big blue stripe, and two small gold stripes on either side of it. Cool, huh?"

I let out a long breath, and stared at my brother. I never figured that getting my own room would be so much work. On TV they just hire some interior designer guy, a work crew comes in, and the room is done in an hour. When I thought of the day ahead of me, one thing that kept me going was knowing that Mitch would be back in New Jersey in just a few days.

# - 7 -

On Sunday night my cell phone rang and I saw it was Mitch. My pulse started to race knowing he was only a few miles away. "When did you get in?" I asked.

"About an hour ago," he said.

"How's your dad?"

"He's okay I guess. It's really been a long summer. He flew down twice. I'll tell you about it later. How about tomorrow? Can we get together and do something?"

"Matt's got the day off and is taking his girlfriend Maggie to the beach. He said we could come. But we'd have to be back early since she has to be at work by six. Maybe you could stay for dinner." For a moment I wondered if I was being too pushy with my plans.

"Sounds great," he said, and I breathed a sigh of relief.

After the phone call ended, the thrill of seeing Mitch in less than a day kept bubbling up in my throat. It would be a great ending to my summer fun. Once hockey practice started Mrs. Fortunato was going to make sure my days were all about hockey.

\*     \*     \*

The next morning I was rummaging through my drawers looking for my bathing suit. My nerves were on overload and my mind was blanking out. After tearing through my bureau for the third time, I finally spotted a glimpse of the dark green fabric of my tankini. As I slipped on the suit and looked in the mirror I saw that I had at least a little color. I hated always being the palest girl on the beach. Throwing on my favorite Billabong T-shirt and khaki shorts, I was set.

"Jackie," my mom called up from the downstairs hall, "make sure you put on sunblock, and don't forget a hat."

*Jeez! I know, I know. I'm not a baby.*

I hated hats, but I had to admit that wearing one between sessions at camp had been a skinsaver. As I stuffed my hat and beach towel into my canvas bag I felt a twinge of doubt about the day. After I had spoken to Mitch, I assumed that everything would be the same as last year, but maybe I was wrong. Maybe once he saw me he would remember how young I looked, and how much of a tomboy I was. I might be a poor comparison to all those Southern girls who knew how to flirt, and dress girly-girl for the guys.

My brother was already at the breakfast table when I got downstairs. "Hey Jack, settle down. I think you're going to explode or something." He laughed.

"Oh, shut up," I said, throwing my napkin at him.

Before we could get into it, the doorbell sounded. I jumped up from the table and hurried to answer it. My hand froze on the doorknob. I had a flashback of freshman year, and my shyness and uncertainty about boys returned.

I took a deep breath, and when I opened the door and saw him, he seemed to be taking up the whole doorway. He was all broad shoulders and long legs. And his hands, I forgot how big they were. I bet he could palm a basketball and baseball at the same time.

"You've grown," I said.

"Is that all you can say, after two months?" he said.

As I stood there, all stupid-like, staring at him, his eyes crinkled in a smile, "So am I invited in or what?"

Feeling the blood rush to my face, I stepped back, "Uh sure."

As he came in he bent down to kiss my cheek and said, "Missed you."

"Me too," I whispered, suddenly feeling a little shy.

We stepped away from each other, neither of us knowing quite what to do next.

"Jackie, bring Mitch out to the kitchen for some breakfast. He must be starved," Mom called from the kitchen.

I gave a silent shout-out to my mom for saving me from this awkward moment and as I started to walk to the kitchen, Mitch touched my arm and said, "Here Jackie, Happy Birthday," and handed me a long gray cardboard tube.

"What's this?" I asked, looking up at him.

"You'll see."

"Jackie!" Mom called again.

"Go on," he said. "You can open it later. Mitch put his gym bag down and followed me into the kitchen where my mom gave him a quick hug welcoming him back. Then Mitch and Matt got lost catching up with guy talk.

Ten minutes later everyone was wolfing down Mom's blueberry waffles, and when we were about finished, Matt looked over at the package sitting next to my chair and asked what it was.

I glanced down at the cardboard tube. "It's a birthday present from Mitch."

"So what's inside?" he asked.

I looked questioningly at Mitch.

"Sure, go ahead. Just pull off the top," Mitch said.

Reaching down I saw it was really like a container used for holding blue prints or posters. I pulled off the top and carefully reached in to slide out the contents. I gasped as I unrolled the paper, and then just looked at Mitch.

"How?" I asked. I was stunned.

Mitch grinned at me. I couldn't believe it and my eyes started to fill up. It was a blown-up picture of my hockey team taken at the end of last season. We were celebrating our victory in the freshman championship. It wasn't one of those posed shots, but a picture of the girls all hugging each other and crying with happiness. In the picture, my face was turned toward the camera, and I looked so happy.

Mom came around to see it, "Oh my, Mitch, this is wonderful."

After I passed the print to my brother, Mitch said, "My dad was taking pictures at the game. We both kind of forgot about it. Later he must have downloaded it, and one day I was scrolling through his slide show and found it. I thought you would like it for your room."

"And I have a new room, too. Now that Matt is a college boy, Mom and Dad are sending him to the basement and I'm getting his room. Want to see it?"

"Sure," Mitch said.

"Don't be long, Matt said. "We have to pick up Maggie in twenty minutes."

Upstairs I felt an incoming wave of the jitters. We were finally going to be alone. I walked to the middle of the room while Mitch stopped in the doorway, watching me. Feeling self-conscious, I pretended to be one of those salesgirls on the Home Shopping Network and stretched my arms wide and twirled around showing off the room.

"Look, no more of Lizzie's Barbie pink," I said, trying to keep the moment light. "What do you think?"

Mitch glanced around the room. "It's great!" he said, but he might have had something on his mind other than wall colors because he crossed the room in two giant strides and pulled me into his arms.

I looked at his wild dark hair that couldn't seem to figure which way it should lay on his head, and took in his soft gray eyes. Then everything fell into place as he kissed me. It was like he never left.

After seconds or minutes, I couldn't be sure which, he took my hand and brought it to his lips, noticing my bracelet for the first time. It was the copper and beaded bracelet that he had given me last Christmas.

"I never take it off, except for sports," I said, as I watched him eyeing the bracelet his mother had made me.

"I'm glad, Jackie." He smiled down at me and tugged gently at one of my curls. "We better get going," he said, "I can't wait to see the ocean."

As we came down the stairs, Matt said it was time to leave. Fifteen minutes later Maggie Brooks, who had been in my brother's class at school and a member of last year's hockey team, slid into the front seat.

# - 8 -

Driving to the beach, the main topic of conversation seemed to be about college. Mitch and Maggie were deep in conversation about her graphic design major when I broke in and asked her if she would still be playing hockey. She said, "Maybe, if I have time."

*Maybe? How could anyone even think about putting their stick down and never play again? Could it really be that easy to do?* I couldn't even imagine it.

Then talk drifted to my brother's soccer scholarship and Mitch's sister, Megan, who was also starting college. My mind kind of went on shutdown. I was more interested in how nice it was to have Mitch sitting alongside of me. Enjoying tenth grade was the most important thing on my personal horizon, and as long as I had hockey and Mitch, I was sure I would.

\* \* \*

There weren't too many people at the beach yet, so we had our pick of places to spread out our towels and blankets. Maggie had brought a cooler with drinks and sandwiches which was something I hadn't even thought about. My mind must have been totally focused on seeing Mitch 'cause I **did** like my munchies.

"Last one in gets dunked," Matt called, as he trotted off to the water's edge. Mitch stripped off his T-shirt, and sprinted down to the water to join Matt. Maggie and I looked at each other.

"You know what this is really about, don't you?" Maggie asked.

"No, what?"

Maggie laughed. "Oh, it's not about getting dunked. It's that they're going to have a long leisurely look at us in our bathing suits while we take our time getting used to the water. And, we just have to let them. It's called 'free ogling,' but we can't really call them on it."

"Okay, we're both fast. Let's give them a short look and dive in right past them," I said, with a grin.

"You're on," she said.

Both of us quickly pulled off our street clothes and raced into the water, splashing the guys as we passed them, and then dived through a wave. When we both reemerged on the other side of the wave, we turned and yelled, "Tie, no dunking."

The four of us spent the next half hour diving through waves and trying to pull each other under. I couldn't remember when I'd had so much fun, and soon we were all exhausted.

Maggie decided she was going back to the blanket to catch some rays and my brother joined her, leaving me and Mitch alone. It felt like we were the only two people in the whole Atlantic Ocean. He reached out and wrapped his arms around me.

"Jackie, you don't know how many times I wanted to have you right next to me this summer."

I smiled up at him thinking pretty much the same thing. Then he took a deep breath, and said, "I need to get some things off my chest. Let's go for a walk, okay?"

The two of us slowly made our way out of the water. I dried off, wondering what was on his mind, and hoping it was nothing about us. I threw on my T-shirt and pulled on my hat, then glanced at Mitch to see if he was going to make a teasing remark about my need to cover up, but his mind seemed somewhere else. He took my hand, and we walked along the water's edge.

"Just how tall have you gotten?" I asked, trying to make small talk.

"Six three."

"You're more than a whole foot taller than me!"

"Yeah, but I watched you racing to the water with Maggie. You make every inch count, believe me."

"I've been lifting weights this summer."

"All I can say is more girls should follow your coaches' training program 'cause you're looking mighty hot there, Reds."

I was relieved that he was starting to come back from wherever his mind had been, but his 'hot' comment kind of embarrassed me. I pushed him toward an oncoming wave and said, "Then maybe you should just cool off."

He pretended to lose his balance and half fell into the water. For a moment it was like we were both back in ninth grade, goofing around and being silly, as if we didn't have a care in the world.

We walked in silence for awhile just holding hands. It was a perfect summer day. One you have to tuck away as a good memory to be taken out later when the cold weather came.

"Jackie, I need to talk to you about this summer," he said, finally.

*Uh-oh.* I wondered what he meant. *Has he been dating someone else, maybe someone in Texas?* I felt a tightening in my stomach, and could feel the clouds forming.

"You know how I decided to come up here with Dad last summer?" he asked.

I nodded, remembering Mitch's explanation for moving from Texas when the military had transferred his dad to New Jersey. Mitch told me he didn't want to have to keep changing schools and was hoping if he started at Northfield as a freshman, he could finish out at the same school.

Mitch stopped walking, turned to face me, and took both of my hands. "Well, my parents made last year's separation seem like just an excuse to let Megan finish out high school in Texas," he said. "It was supposed to be just a temporary thing. I knew things had been a little tense when my dad came home from his last assignment overseas. He had been away for two months, but I thought things would blow over. Maybe I was just hoping."

I could feel his tension in my hands. He paused for a moment like he didn't want to continue, yet knew he had to.

"To make a long story short they're separating for good," he said.

He looked at me, waiting for me to say something. For a moment I honestly felt relieved, that it wasn't about some girl. Then I felt guilty that my initial reaction had been so selfish. The idea of my own parents splitting up was unimaginable. I knew divorce happened, of course, but not to anyone close to me. The words just spilled out of me, "Mitch, I'm so sorry," but I knew they weren't enough. What was?

"Jackie, I look at your mom and dad, and they seem so happy. I can't understand why my parents can't be like that. He bent down and picked up a shell, turned it over, and then heaved it as far as he could out into the water. "My mom isn't giving my dad a chance," he said. "I mean she knew he was in the military when they got married. Now she says she needs to stop being a vagabond and wants her own life. My dad retires in less than a year. Why can't she wait?"

I had no answer for him, and wasn't sure he even expected one. I couldn't get my head around the whole thing. "What do your sisters think?" I finally asked.

"My oldest sister just says 'they have to do what they have to do,' whatever that means. Megan is more upset. But I think she kind of takes Mom's side. Her college is close to where my mom has an apartment, so she'll come home when she can. See, we sold our house and now Mom has her own place. You always called my cell phone so you couldn't realize what happened."

"Why didn't you tell me about all this?"

"I don't know. It was all messed up. My only break was going to basketball camp for two weeks. That's what kept me from going totally nuts. That, and knowing you were back here, too," he said.

I gave his hand a squeeze. I wanted to reassure him that everything would be all right, but couldn't. Maybe it was me who wanted reassurance. It was a sad conversation. Instead, I said what I thought he wanted to hear, and what I wished for.

"Maybe your parents will miss each other and change their minds," I said.

"I don't really see that happening, but I hope you're right. Anyway that's the deal in the Kennedy family right now."

I thought about what he'd just told me and the other kids I knew that didn't have two parents living together. There was Lindsay, of course. Her Dad had died when she was only a baby. Then there was a girl on my team who lived with her grandparents. Her parents just took off one day. Still, when it happened to somebody you cared about, and, so unexpected, the news kind of blows you over. It was a scary feeling.

Pulling myself away from these thoughts, I said, "So you've decided to stay with your dad, right?"

"Yeah, I don't think I could live with my mother right now. I'm pretty ticked. Besides, my dad will need me more than ever."

We stopped and turned back. To be honest, I wished in a way that Mitch had never told me any of it, like it never happened, and everything could be the same as it was before. It was just too big.

Mitch interrupted my thoughts, "Thanks for hearing me out, Jackie."

He put his arm around my shoulder and kept me close as we walked back to the blankets. We didn't talk much, and I was feeling guilty about the way my thinking was going, like I didn't really understand what he was going through, and couldn't really help anyway.

Matt looked up from the blanket when he saw us coming. "Hey, where have you two been? Maggie and I were going to call the lifeguards and have them do a search and rescue," he said, kiddingly.

"Believe it or not this is my first trip to the Atlantic Ocean. I just wanted to take it all in, you know?" Mitch said.

"Right," Matt said, and I caught him scowling a bit as he checked out Mitch's arm tightly wrapped around me.

\*　　\*　　\*

The beach was starting to get more crowded, but it wasn't like midsummer with its usual wall-to-wall blankets and chairs. A lot of people had already left the shore behind for back-to-school shopping or college.

"I'm starved," I said, eager to shift the day to a happier topic.

"Aren't you always?" Matt asked.

I made a face at him. "I don't see you going on any diet," I teased back.

"Hey, I have to beef up for pre-season. It's supposed to be a killer."

"When do you start?" Mitch asked as he dug into a sandwich.

"Our parents are taking me to school on Friday and we have our first session that night. I've already talked to my roommate. He's a soccer player, too, from New York State. He got all excited when he found out I only lived an hour from school so I sort of had to promise him some of Mom's Saturday night dinners."

For awhile we just chilled out enjoying the lunch that Maggie packed. It was just the break I needed to push Mitch's problems to the back of my mind.

"Maggie, this is great. Mitch and I really appreciate it," I said, shooing a seagull that was eyeing our bag of chips.

"I thought it would be fun to have a picnic on the beach," she said. "It's got to hold me a long time. I probably won't see the beach again 'til next summer."

It suddenly hit me what going away to college really meant. A year was a long time. I was sure glad I had a couple of years not to have to think about stuff like that. I grabbed the tube of sunblock and told Mitch I'd had enough of the ocean for awhile. The sea air and sun were making me sleepy, but he was still up for more waves. I stretched out on the blanket and squirmed around for a comfortable position in the sand. Then I closed my eyes.


When I woke, and turned my head, I saw Mitch lying next to me. He seemed to be asleep. I realized that my legs were covered with a towel. I wondered if Mitch had done this for me 'cause I could have been fried by now. I lifted my head and looked around, but Matt and Maggie had disappeared.

I rolled over on my side and watched Mitch's steady breathing. He was lying on his stomach, his head turned toward me. It was rare that I could study him like this without feeling self-conscious. My gaze wandered over him, and I realized he must have been lifting this summer, too, 'cause he was way more muscular than most boys I knew. He was such a good athlete. I remembered the times I watched his basketball team play last winter. He was super quick for being so tall, and he moved with such grace. I know you aren't supposed to use a word like that about a boy, but, really, there was no other way to describe him, and he made playing the game look so easy.

I glanced back to his face, and one gray eye popped open.

"Whatcha see there, Reds?"

Embarrassed at being caught out, I stammered, "Noth… nothing, just wondered if you were awake."

He gave me a lazy smile. "Uh-huh."

*Drat, caught at my own ogling.* Quickly changing the subject I said, "Was it you who covered up my legs?" He nodded.

"Gee, thanks, I could have been toast."

"We can't have that," he said, grinning at me.

Our moment alone was interrupted by Maggie as she and Matt were jogging toward us, "Hey, you two come on with us. We found something really neat."

"What is it?" I asked, starting to stand.

"Hurry up before they leave," Matt called, impatiently.

# - 9 -

The four of us jogged about a quarter mile to a more deserted section of the beach where there weren't any lifeguards. We saw three guys and a girl, with these funny sticks that kind of looked like butterfly nets on a diet. They were throwing a yellow ball through the air.

I recognized it at once. It was lacrosse. We didn't have the sport at our school, but I had seen it on TV.

*How can they catch with that thing? They make it look so easy.* I was fascinated and itchy to try it.

Matt went up to one of the guys and started asking a ton of questions.

The boy was surprised we didn't play it, and Maggie explained our conference was a little backwards, but she had heard we were going to start a program.

"We'll show you how," the boy said, and for the next half hour the eight of us took turns moving the ball in the sticks and trying to throw and catch to each other. It was harder than it looked.

"Hey, go long," one boy said to Matt. My brother took off down the beach, and the boy threw him a long, lobbed pass. At the last minute Matt reached up and snagged the ball out of the air.

"Awesome," he yelled.

"Can I try one?" I asked. I was dying to see if I could do it.

"Sure," the girl said. I sprinted away from her, and the girl arched the ball in the air over my left shoulder. Just as the ball was about to hit the sand, I reached out, scooped the ball into the stick, and continued running down the beach with it.

"Good catch," called the girl.

After everyone had a few more tries, we turned to go, and thanked them for letting us try it out. Walking back to the blankets, Maggie explained that she had overheard the coaches talking about starting a lacrosse club next spring.

My mind started buzzing. "Do you think they'd take a beginner?"

"Probably everybody would be a beginner," she said.

I was thinking maybe I'd give it a try. It looked like fun and would sure give me something to do in the spring when there was no hockey. I was definitely going to tell the twins about it.

*       *       *

Soon it was time to pack up. After we left Maggie off, I asked Mitch again if he wanted to stay for dinner, and maybe invite his father, too. I didn't want the day to end.

Two hours later we were all enjoying a typical McKendry clan barbecue. In a quiet moment I said what had been buzzing about in my mind. "Guess what? We saw a new game at the beach today. It's called lacrosse. Maggie said the school's going to start a program next spring."

Major Kennedy looked up from his plate. "It's a pretty wild sport, Jackie, lots of action."

That sounded pretty good to me, especially 'the lots of action' part.

After dinner, as I was walking Mitch out to the car, he whispered to me, "I'll call you tomorrow night, and thanks for listening."

I stood on the front steps watching them drive away, and as their car got smaller and smaller I realized I had so much fun at the beach that I had almost forgotten what Mitch had told me about his parents. My summer had to have been so much easier than his. It was almost like we had been living in two different worlds, and I wasn't just thinking of Texas and New Jersey. Turning to go inside, I wondered if my mom and dad knew about the separation.

*   *   *

I found my brother busy writing away at the kitchen table. I peered over his shoulder and saw that he was making a list of what he needed to take to school.

"Hey, thanks again for letting us come to the beach with you guys today," I said.

He nodded and kept on writing. He came to the end of the page and threw his pen down. I thought he was done, but he picked up the pen again and turned to face me. He didn't look at me. Instead, he studied the pen like he was searching for something.

"Listen, Jack," he said, "I'm going to be gone soon, and you're going to be on your own at school and all ... and well, just remember, you're only a sophomore, so don't rush things. Okay?"

"What do you mean?"

"I like Mitch, don't get me wrong, but sometimes I think he is a little too intense. You know, as you get older a lot of guys are going to hit on you."

"What are you saying? Don't you think he likes me?" I could feel some giant hand clutching my chest, and all my muscles tightening. I didn't understand where all this was coming from.

"Sure he likes you, a lot I think, but he's your first boyfriend. Just be careful and don't get too serious. That's all."

*What? What does he mean? He can't really be trying to have "the talk." Jeez, Mom and I went over that one long ago.*

"Well, what about you and Maggie?" I snapped back at him, my temper flaring.

"I'm not talking about me and Maggie. I'm talking about you," he said, throwing some heat of his own.

Matt could see I was getting upset. He said more quietly, "Look, Jackie, it's just that I was watching him with you and I couldn't leave without saying anything. I don't want you to get in over your head. Even though you're a little punk, I want you to be okay."

Before I could say anything, Mom came into the kitchen and looked at the two of us.

"What's going on? You both look so serious."

I blinked away some tears that had somehow found their way into the corners of my eyes, turned my back on them both, and walked over to the fridge to get a drink.

I heard Matt say, "Oh, we were just talking about the new school year."

As I took a sip of juice, I remembered the awkward conversation I had with Matt, almost a year ago, when he and his old girlfriend had broken up and he was such a mess.

*Is this some sort of payback, getting in my face? Mitch and I are just fine. Butt out, Matt.*

I carefully put the glass in the sink, buying myself some time. Feeling a little more in control, I turned and leaned against the sink.

"Yeah, Matt just reminded me about how much I'm going to miss him when he goes away to school," I said.

Matt must have figured it was all okay 'cause he said, "Sure, no more free rides to school in the morning."

I gave him a weak smile, "Well, I better get to bed. Night, Mom. See you tomorrow, Matt."

It was hard getting to sleep that night. *What the heck happened to the day? It started out so great. Then Mitch told me about his family, and then my brother drops this 'don't grow up too fast' talk on me. Really, if everything could be like last year, life would be fine.* Everything around me seemed to be changing shape and the world was spinning faster. I needed an anchor, something that wouldn't change.

# - 10 -

"Tonight I thought we would run out to the mall and look for curtains and a bedspread for your new room," Mom said the next morning. "How about it?"

"Great," I said. It was just what I needed, something that would keep my mind off last night's conversation with Matt. I walked over to help Mom unload the dishwasher and asked, "Did you know Mitch's parents have separated?"

She turned to me and carefully put the dishes she was holding down on the counter.

"He told me yesterday at the beach," I added.

"How's Mitch doing with it, honey?"

I reached into the bottom of the dishwasher for the remaining plates. "He tries to be okay, but I think he's upset. He feels his mother really let the family down," I said.

"Well, Jackie, marriages are very complex relationships. It's usually not a question of one person being right and one person being wrong."

"I guess, but I really feel bad for Mitch."

"Me too, honey. This could be a very trying time for all of the Kennedys."

My mom kind of dropped it there but I couldn't, and nothing she said really made me feel any better. I definitely needed a break from all my heavy-duty thinking, and playing hockey with my two best friends seemed like the perfect answer.

\*     \*     \*

The twins and I hurried through our stick work drills, and then started our run through the park.

At the end of the first mile, Tori, still breathing easy, asked, "So Jackie, how's your boy?" She laughed. "Sparks still flying?"

I felt the color come into my cheeks, but quickly got to what was on my mind. "I don't know, I mean, I was really glad to see him and all. We spent yesterday at the beach, but he's had a tough summer. His parents have split up."

Jules almost stopped her running, but saw me still moving so she sped up again. "That's terrible, how's he doing?" she asked.

"He's trying hard to be okay, but I'm not so sure. Look, don't say anything to him. If he wants to tell people about it, that's up to him, okay?"

"Sure, no problem," Tori said.

But it was a problem. I just didn't know how much of one.

\*     \*     \*

After dinner Mom and I went to the mall. We found a great chocolate-brown comforter in a wild geometric print. I loved it. Next we stopped at a frame store and had my birthday gift from Mitch framed and mounted. I was psyched when I saw the result. The photograph looked even better. My new room was definitely shaping up.

Driving home I asked Mom if Matt was still okay about giving up his room.

"He's fine with it. Really, he's so wound up about soccer and college that he can barely think of anything else. This weekend we'll move all your things into your new room, and get you settled before school starts."

Later I found Matt in his room taping up a box for school. I glanced around the room. It seemed a little sad, like it somehow knew it was being abandoned. Studying the empty walls, I gave them a silent shout-out not to worry, 'cause I was going to make them look terrific again.

Matt pushed the box against the wall, and when he straightened up, he said, "Oh yeah, I forgot, Mitch called a couple of times. He said something about not being able to reach you on your cell phone."

It suddenly dawned on me that I didn't have the phone with me, and wondered for a moment just how convenient it was that Matt had forgotten Mitch's calls. I raced down the hall to my room sending a mental message to my brother to stay out of it and not cause problems between me and Mitch.

I found my phone under a pile of clothes on the floor. Grabbing it, I thought I better put 'cell phone' on my things to remember list since it sure took me long enough to get it.

I sat down on the edge of the bed and I checked my messages. Two were from Mitch wanting to know where I was, and a third was from Jules, asking me to call her.

*Mitch first.* "Hey, Mom and I were at the mall and I forgot my cell phone," I said. "Sorry."

"I thought you were ducking me, Jackie."

"Why would I do that?" I sat up straighter, puzzled at his comment.

"The beach – you know, what we talked about."

"Why would stuff about your parents matter?"

"I don't know. Thinking too much, I guess. I need school to start and just forget about the summer."

I began to pace around the room. I tried to reassure him that everything would be okay. But the words sounded kind of empty, even to my own ears. It felt like I was throwing a bunch of stupid words in the air, just because I knew I was supposed to say something. It made me feel dumb being so young and not knowing the right answers.

I stopped my pacing when Mitch asked me to a movie on Saturday night. I thought that maybe he needed a break, maybe more than I did, and decided a movie would be good for both of us.

After we hung up I thought about the whole conversation. It wasn't like him at all. He'd always been so confident and playful with me. Speed dialing Jules' number, I thought that this 'parents breaking up' thing messed with a lot of people's heads. It was **so** not fair.

"Hey Jules, what's going on?" I asked, relieved to be ending my thoughts about Mitch's family.

"Did you get your schedule?" she asked.

"No, not yet," I said.

"Tori and I have English class together which is cool." She laughed, "Somebody slipped up somewhere," referring to her parents not wanting her and her sister to have any classes together.

"You know, I never checked the mail today. Maybe I got my schedule, too. Hold on," I said, as I raced downstairs. I found a pile of letters on the hall table, and sorted through the pieces of mail 'til I came to one with my name on it.

I slumped into a living room chair and tore open the envelope. "Whoa, Jules, I got honors English and honors history." I was psyched. All that work really paid off last year. Maybe I wasn't a total classroom idiot after all.

"Okay, the important stuff, my homeroom is A112," I said.

"Great, mine too," Jules said. "What else?"

"Okay, first period is Spanish II, second geometry, third history, and then physical education."

Jules broke in, "Hey, I have phys ed at the same time. Who's your teacher?"

"Let me look, oh here, a Mr. Rose. Who's he?"

"He coaches tennis. I have him too. Gym is going to be so much fun."

"I have lunch next," I said.

"Well, at least you and Tori will be together. I have lunch sixth. What's the rest of your schedule?"

"English, biology, and then study hall," I said. "I'll miss you at lunch, Jules, but I'm glad we have something together."

"Me, too. You know Ellen is in our homeroom, too, and she has lunch with you and Tori. We already checked."

I started to walk upstairs as we continued our conversation, happy that I knew all this stuff about school. Then I remembered someone.

"How about Lindsay?" I asked.

"I don't know. I didn't find out."

"Oh," I said, then I changed the subject. "Our first day will be a lot different than last year. Remember sitting in that crowded auditorium last year and being scared to death? Maybe tenth grade will be a breeze."

"Maybe. Listen, I have to go, but my mother wants me to remind you that she'll pick you up at 7:30 Thursday morning. Okay?"

"Yep, I'll be ready. Enjoy your last pain-free day, Jules."

She laughed and said, "You, too."

# - 11 -

Even though classes don't start for another two weeks, the first day of practice with the coaches means the beginning of the next school year for most fall athletes. Despite the heat and humidity of August, you're rising early to meet with your teammates and coaches ready for the new season. Your heartbeat quickens. Everything you train for is about to be tested, and your hopes are high for all the days ahead.

That was exactly how I felt as I grabbed an energy bar, water, and a banana on Thursday morning, and slipped out the front door to wait for my ride. I sat on the front steps having a quiet breakfast and tried to imagine what practice would be like. The more I thought about it, the more my foot started tapping. I was relieved when Mrs. Hanson's blue Caddie pulled up so my leg could have a rest.

As soon as I slid in the back with Jules, Tori turned around in the front seat and gave me her boo-hoo face. "I think I'm on my way to an execution," she said.

Jules gave Tori's seat a push. "Stop it. You're being a baby."

"Girls," said Mrs. Hanson, "Jackie doesn't want to hear squabbling. Good morning, Jackie," she said and smiled at me in the rearview mirror.

It was an awfully quiet ride to school. I guessed I wasn't the only one worked up about what the first day of practice might be like. It didn't get any livelier as we made our way across the parking lot to the fields either.

Finally Tori said, "Am I going to survive this?" I gave her a slight grin, but it felt kind of forced and sure didn't reach my whole face.

"Did you ever see any headlines about a Northfield player dying from hard work?" Jules asked.

I think she was getting a little fed up with her sister.

"Well, there are such things as heat stroke and dehydration," Tori pouted.

When we reached the entrance to the field, I put my arm around Tori's waist. "I promise, we won't let that big bad woman do anything life-threatening," I said, referring of course to Mrs. Fortunato, Northfield's Head Coach.

"Okay," Tori laughed, "I'm going to hold you to that."

I glanced back at Jules, and noticed that Ms. Gillespie, the assistant coach, was walking right next to her. Ms. Gillespie must have felt my gaze 'cause she gave Tori and me a long look. Then she turned to go toward the locker room. *Had she overheard us talking? What if she tells Mrs. Fortunato about my big bad woman comment? Can this day start out any worse?*

*       *       *

A couple dozen players were already hitting around, and still more were coming in through the gate behind us. Since we had a few minutes before practice officially started, Tori grabbed a ball, and asked me to hit with her, while Jules walked over and started talking to one of our old teammates.

Off in the distance, I noticed Mrs. Fortunato coming out of the locker room deep in conversation with Ms. Gillespie. I was so caught up in watching them moving toward us, wondering what they were talking about, that I didn't see Tori smash a ball at me, and it hit my knee.

"Ow, that hurts."

Tori grinned. "Sorry. Maybe someone should be taking care of you, instead."

I was thinking that maybe Tori should look up before she hits, but held my tongue.

Promptly at eight o'clock, Mrs. Fortunato blew her whistle. For a second I cringed, imagining that I would hear my name called out as an early cut 'cause of my big mouth. Instead Coach announced we were doing Northfield's traditional beginning of the season test – the three-mile timed run. The course would start at our field, wind through the neighboring development, and end back at the school.

Lining up for the start, I looked around at the other girls. Some faces showed worry, others were focused. A few girls were kidding around, but you could hear the nervousness coming through their laughter. I was nervous, too, but also relieved that if she had done anything, Ms. Gillespie didn't rat me out to Mrs. Fortunato.

On our coach's signal, we were off. Most of the sophomores stayed in a pack for the first mile. Jules, who was riding my shoulder, said, "Jackie, we need to pick up the pace. We're starting to fall behind some of the others. This is a competition and we need to do our best."

I wasn't sure whether it was better to stay with our friends or push myself and try to match the older girls, but Jules' urging won out, and I said, "Okay, let's go."

By the end of the second mile, we'd passed half of the upperclassmen, and Becky had caught up to Jules and me.

"It's about time you two decided to push it. I was getting bored back there waiting for someone to make a move."

Jules and I laughed. Becky had always been the number one runner in our class back in elementary school which was kind of cool for a goalkeeper. It would be kind of interesting to see how she'd match up with the older girls.

With half a mile to go, there were Becky, Jules, and me, and two of the upperclassmen, Mandy and Kat, at the front. The final two hundred yards became a five-girl sprint. As we ran through the empty parking lot toward the open gate that was the finish line, Jules and Kat started to fade.

*I can't beat Mandy. It wouldn't look right. I don't want her mad and have more trouble with the upperclassmen.*

I purposely slowed my pace just enough so that Becky, who was now in the lead, and Mandy, could slide through the gate ahead of me.

"Good job," Mrs. Fortunato called to us as Ms. Gillespie wrote down our scores. We were walking it off when Jules came over to me.

"How come you put the brakes on?" she said. "Maybe none of us could have beaten Becky, but coming in second would have been great for you."

I looked at the frown on Jules' face and shrugged my shoulders. "I don't know," I said, but I could see from Jules' expression that she didn't get what I did.

At the end of practice, we were walking toward the parking lot and Tori said, "That wasn't so bad, but I think I need to take a nap this afternoon."

Jules put her arm around Tori. "Honestly I'm proud of you, sister. I thought you did great."

My mom was there waiting for us and we piled in the back of the car. Lizzie, who was sitting in the front seat, turned around, "Ugh, you all smell yucky!"

"Lizzie, mind your manners and turn around," Mom said. Then she looked in the rearview mirror, "Girls, don't mind Lizzie. How was it?"

"We're all kind of glad it's over, but going to camp really helped us a lot," I said.

"Oh, I don't know about that," Tori said. "I don't think Ken prepared me for this at all."

"Who's Ken?" I asked searching my mind for some new boy in Tori's life that I didn't know about.

Jules laughed. "That's Tori's pet name for her coach at camp. Don't you remember the tall blonde guy that looked like he spent all his time on a surfboard? Tori told me he reminded her of her old Barbie doll's boyfriend, hence, the name."

"Tori, you're special," I said, and gave her a nudge.

Mom interrupted our goofiness, "I bet you all are famished. How about a trip to the Pancake Palace for some brunch? It'll be my treat."

Lizzie gave a squeal of delight, and I'm pretty sure if the rest of us hadn't been so tired we might have been squealing, too.

\*     \*     \*

I was going to pass right by my brother's room, but something made me stop and I leaned against the door frame to watch him work. He was dividing up his stuff, some to go to the basement and other things being labeled for school. Suddenly I couldn't hold onto my mad.

"It's going to seem strange with you away at school," I said.

"Right," he said, barely glancing at me.

"So, are you going out with Maggie tonight?"

"Yep, nosy, one more time. Then I probably won't see her 'til Christmas."

"Won't that be sad?"

He finally stopped what he was doing and looked over his shoulder at me. "Sure I'll miss Maggie, she's a great girl, but we plan to date other people in college, so whatever happens, happens."

I was surprised by his answer and started to turn away.

"Look, Maggie and I agreed on this long ago. So don't look so bummed. You're being way too romantic," he said.

I left him to finish what he was doing. I couldn't get over how people could just walk away after dating for so long. I wondered if that would happen to Mitch and me someday, then thought who was to say we'd even last that long.

\*     \*     \*

I decided to call Mitch after dinner, explaining that I was tired and needed to get up early to say good-bye to Matt.

"I forgot he's leaving tomorrow. Is he excited?" he asked.

I sat down on my bed and pulled off my socks and sneakers. "He can't wait."

"So was it a killer out there today?"

I finally laughed and gave him the lowdown. Then I asked him if he got his schedule.

"Yep, I'm in C124 for homeroom and I have sixth period lunch. What about you?"

"I have homeroom with Jules in A wing and fifth lunch. Tell me the rest of your schedule." When he did, we found out that the only time we would see each other was in gym class.

"It'll seem funny that I won't see you as much as I did last year," I said.

"Yeah, I know, but at least we have gym, and besides, we're together now so the hard part is over."

"What do you mean the hard part?" I asked, picking up the framed photo of Mitch and me that was sitting on my desk.

"Reds, do you have any idea how hard it was for me to get you to even think I didn't have two heads?"

I put the photograph back in its place and said. "I don't know about the two heads part. I just wasn't sure I wanted to get involved with anyone."

"And are you glad you did?"

"Most days ... just kidding, yes, very glad."

"Me, too. Well, I'll let you go. Good luck in practice and tell Matt I said good-bye."

*     *     *

The next morning I was up and dressed by seven o'clock. I crept into my brother's room and found him asleep. I leaned down to whisper his name and he groaned.

"What's up?" he asked, still half asleep.

"I just wanted to say good-bye and wish you luck."

He reached out and fisted my shoulder, "Thanks, Jack. Good luck with hockey. You're in the big leagues now, so go get 'em."

"I will. I have to go ... and thanks for my new room," I said, as I moved toward the door.

"Right," he mumbled, then rolled over and fell right back to sleep.

Going down the stairs, I pictured my brother sitting in some train that was moving out of the station. In my imagination, he wasn't looking back at the rest of us who were standing on the platform. Instead, he was looking straight ahead, like we didn't even exist. It was kind of weird how you could have thoughts rambling through your head like that. But Matt had always been there for me, making sure I was safe at school, and then later when I played in the park he would always be checking on me, making sure the bigger kids weren't picking on me. And, now he was leaving. He seemed so happy. I wished I could just be happy for him.

While I was having breakfast, Mom walked into the kitchen reminding me to pick up Lizzie at our neighbor's after practice since she and my dad were taking Matt to his college and wouldn't be home until dinnertime.

"I'm going to miss Matt," I said. "It was fun to go out with him and Maggie. It was almost like he wasn't just my brother, but a friend, too, you know, and now he's leaving."

She walked over and gave me a hug. "I understand, honey, but as you both get older you and Matt will always be there for each other." I thought 'when we were older' seemed a long way off. My mind was more on today, maybe next week.

Mom walked away and opened a canister to make the coffee for my dad. Then she turned to me. "Dad and I will miss him, too, you know. I'll let you in on a secret, woman to woman."

When she said that, I stopped my grazing, and sat up a little straighter.

"Part of me will always think of him as my baby boy, taking his first hesitant little steps. To let him go is hard for me, too, just for different reasons," she said.

I didn't know what to say. I felt like my mom had just opened up some adult window and let me peek inside. Picking up my spoon to finish my cereal, I got a flash of me standing on a train platform, and waving to a little girl, and she was not looking back at me either.

\*     \*     \*

The morning's practice was hard with some killer conditioning, but I kind of thrived on the physical work, plus it took my mind off Matt leaving. I tried to watch some of the older players and see if I could copy what they were doing. I noticed a few of the sophomores who hadn't been to camp start to wilt. The only one who didn't was Sam Jones. I thought she must have worked awfully hard on her own to hang like she was, and I wondered if I would have been so ready without the twins and camp to prepare me.

On my way home I picked up Lizzie, started making her lunch, and then my cell phone rang. It was Mitch.

"Hey, I'm playing Top Chef with the peanut butter and jelly jars," I said, trying to keep the phone to my ear as I finished the sandwich. The phone slipped and I missed what he was saying. "Oops, sorry, about that," I said when I picked the phone up again, "Lizzie was starving from all her hard work watching TV at the neighbor's this morning." Lizzie made a face at me and I laughed back at her as I put her sandwich in front of her.

"Uh-oh, I don't think she liked my effort," I said, as I tickled Lizzie under her ribs.

Lizzie shrieked laughing, "Stop, Jackie!"

And I heard "Stop, Jackie" echoing from the phone.

Puzzled, I walked away from Lizzie, and plopped down in a chair at the other end of the kitchen table.

"What's the matter?" I asked into the phone.

"It was ... I don't know." He paused, then said, "Actually, I called to check with you about Saturday, but it sounds as if you're busy. I mean, that is, if you still want to go."

"Of course I do. Why would you even think that?" I asked, shifting in my chair, trying to understand where the conversation was going.

There was silence for a moment, and then he said, "I'm sorry, Jackie. I don't know what's the matter with me."

He seemed on edge, and I wondered how I would be if my parents told me they were splitting up. It had to be like someone blowing up your future, and no one giving you any direction on what you were supposed to do next. Was I expected to be the one to help him figure it out? I just turned fifteen. I couldn't even find a way to get my mom off my back about sports.

Mitch broke into my thoughts. "My dad said he can take us and pick us up. Is it all right if we go with Davey and his girlfriend?"

"Sure," I answered, remembering Davey Barr, a boy on the wrestling team, who dated Tori for a few months last year. "Who's he going out with?"

"Someone from St. Benedict's. I don't know her."

"I think the last time I spoke to him was when he and Tori broke up," I said, and walked over to the fridge for something to drink.

"Well, Tori didn't let any grass grow under her feet when she started going out with that soccer player," Mitch said, coming to his friend's defense.

"Mitch, that's not fair. Tori liked Davey a lot. Remember they had that huge fight? Tori will still not talk about it. She only went out with the soccer player to make Davey jealous. It just didn't help."

"Yeah, you're right, I totally forgot about that. Oh," he said, almost like he just remembered, "my mother sent me another email last night."

*This is so hard. How can anything be solved when his mother is so far away?*

"How is she?" I asked, as I rummaged through the fridge looking for something good.

"She seems excited. Her business is picking up. She says her jewelry is featured in ten gift stores now in Texas. She can't keep up with the orders."

"Well, that's good isn't it?" I asked, as I grabbed a can of lemonade.

"I guess. I just wish she didn't sound so happy. I don't think she misses my dad at all."

"I bet she misses you, though," I said, remembering the conversation I had with my mom this morning about Matt.

"Maybe. Anyway, my dad says he is taking a few days off next week and we're going camping together, somewhere in Western New York."

"That'll be great, Mitch. Maybe you just need to have time for you and your dad to talk. Maybe you can do it when you're away. Are you going to fish?"

"Try to," he said, and I could finally catch some happiness in his voice.

At that moment he sounded like the old Mitch and my heart kind of melted. I **so** wanted to reverse the clock and have my old, carefree boyfriend back.

*     *     *

Around 5:30 Mom and Dad pulled into the driveway. "We're home," Mom called, as she came in the back door, "and we brought Chinese."

"Yea," cheered my sister, and I threw a 'second' Mom's way.

My mom gave Lizzie a peck on the top of her head, and then came over to me and gave me a quick hug. "It was a long day, Jackie. I just couldn't face making a meal."

While we were all sitting around the table, my mom and dad were telling me about their day.

"We met his roommate," Mom said. "He seemed like a nice boy."

This meant practically nothing, of course, just something parents said unless the person had ten piercings, blue hair, and tattoos running down their arms.

"The boys were very excited about their first practice, which is," Dad said looking at his watch, "just about now."

Mom said, half laughingly, "He barely saw us leave, he was so keyed up." Her voice sounded a little scratchy, like she had caught a cold. I looked up and saw her eyes filled with tears, and then I noticed Dad reach out to take Mom's hand. The gesture seemed to make her feel better, and I saw Mom turn her hand over, grab Dad's hand, and hold it tight.

Two thoughts ran through my mind, almost at the same time. I wondered if they'd miss me as much if I went away to school. The second, more important one was, someday I want to be loved like my dad loves my mom.

# - 12 -

The next morning I looked up from my cereal and noticed my mom moving around the kitchen like a robot whose wiring had short-circuited somehow. She rinsed the kitchen sink three different times, then opened and closed the refrigerator door twice, without anything going in or coming out. It was **so** not my organized Mom.

Finally she must have realized that I was staring at her. "I need to keep busy today. This afternoon we'll move your things into your new bedroom," she said, as she repositioned the magnets on the refrigerator door.

"Mom, it'll be okay. You'll be going to his games and even if he doesn't play you'll still see him. Look, if you want, I'll go and get my nails done with you this week."

Mom stopped what she was doing and turned to look at me. "I love you, Jackie McKendry. I know we don't always agree on everything, but I think you're an incredibly special girl," she said.

*Don't agree on everything? That's a mild understatement.* I smiled at her, trying to be cool, but my mind was racing. *At least you think I'm special. But wait, that could mean in a bad way, like I'm the weird one.*

That's the way I usually thought. I always figured that somehow I was a bit of a disappointment to my mom, kind of floating between Matt (Mr. Stud-Athlete), and Lizzie (The Little Princess). But maybe, just maybe, she liked me too. Don't get me wrong, I knew she loved me, but when a parent likes you, sometimes, that's even better.

*　　*　　*

At practice Mrs. Fortunato announced we would be scrimmaging that day. She put me on a forward line with Sam Jones and another sophomore, but our defending teammates were mostly upperclassmen. When I lined up for the start, I looked down the field toward the goal, and saw that I'd be playing against Lindsay, Heather, and Jules. It seemed really weird 'cause I was always used to them playing with me when it really mattered, like now.

I almost laughed out loud the first time I moved the ball toward goal, and saw Jules coming at me with a serious expression on her face. All my happy thoughts stopped a moment later when Jules stripped me of the ball, and I was left standing all by myself, the ball going the other way down the field.

*What's up Jules? That's not funny!* Then I realized that Jules meant business, and she had just embarrassed me in front of Mrs. Fortunato. I could feel the steam rising.

The next time I got the ball I went right at Jules. I remembered the fake I learned at camp. Jules totally committed to it, and I left her in the dust. I passed off to Sam at the edge of the circle, and Sam slammed the ball into the goal cage.

When Mrs. Fortunato made substitutions, Jules and I found ourselves sitting alone at the end of the bench. Jules looked at me, trying to get my attention, but I just stared straight ahead ignoring her.

"Jeez, Jackie, it's a competition, nothing personal."

I sat there for a moment not saying anything. Then slowly I turned to look at her. She could see in my eyes how wound up I was.

"Think about it, wouldn't you want me to play my best, wouldn't you want me to push you to do your best?" she said.

My shoulders sagged, and I stared down at the ground. "You're right," I said, finally. "I was just surprised, that's all."

She crossed one leg over her knee, started to clean out some grass that was stuck to her cleats, then stopped. "Jackie, what do you want?" she asked. "What're you willing to fight for?"

"What do you mean?" I said, irritated at her questions. "I want to make the team."

"I think you should be aiming a little higher. I am," she said.

"Like what?"

Jules looked around, then lowered her voice, "I want to make varsity. They lost a lot of people to graduation, so there are going to be openings."

"I just thought our class would all be together and play JV," I said. "I mean, it would be cool if the varsity was crushing a team and maybe Coach would put us in to get experience, but that's a long shot."

Jules shook her head. "Jackie, you need to think about this. You've really got talent. You should use it."

"I work hard," I snapped.

The whistle blew for substitutions. Our names were called and as we jogged back out on the field, Jules turned to me and said, "That's not what I mean and you know it."

The next fifteen minutes on the field were a blur. All I thought about was Jules getting on my case, and making my thinking about hockey all complicated.

\*     \*     \*

Waiting for Mom to pick us up, Jules started up again. Tori interrupted her sister, "What's up with you two?"

Jules turned to Tori, "I think we all need to figure out what we want from hockey."

"Well, I want to have a good time, that's it," Tori said.

"I know that's what you think you want and that's your choice, Tori," Jules said. "Jackie needs to know what she wants."

I looked down at the ground. *What do I want?*

Our conversation was put on hold when Mom pulled up in the car. Piling into the back seat, Jules said, "Jackie, we're having a barbecue tomorrow. How about coming over for dinner?"

I really hated when Jules and I disagreed on stuff. Her opinions really mattered. I decided that maybe going over to her house might help me figure things out, so I gave an okay to the dinner invitation.

After we left the twins off, Mom said, "I've cleaned out Matt's things and boxed what he doesn't need right now, so we have plenty of space to get things organized. Let's get your room together. Then next week I'll start working on curtains, and then next month I'll tackle Lizzie's room."

"Boy, you have it all mapped out. Maybe you should be in Major Kennedy's military outfit," I said.

"Keeping busy takes my mind off things," she said, then quickly changed the subject. "Speaking of the Kennedys, don't you have a date with Mitch tonight?"

"Uh-huh," I said. "We're going to the movies with Davey Barr and his girlfriend. Mitch will be away next week with his dad. I think they're going camping, maybe some fishing, too."

Mom glanced over at me. "That will probably be good for both of them. How **is** Mitch anyway?" she asked, as she turned into our driveway.

I looked out the side window, a bit lost for words, and then I decided to say what was on my mind. "He's different."

"How so?" Mom asked, always on parent alert.

"I don't know, like sometimes he is the old cheerful Mitch, full of fun, you know, real upbeat. But sometimes he seems so serious, and so … I guess you would say … lost."

"Jackie, it's going to take some time for him to accept that his parents might not stay married. Something like that can throw somebody's world upside down, but I'm sure they both love Mitch, so it'll work out in time. Come on, we have a bedroom to fill."

*　　*　　*

That night, as I was getting ready for my date, I gave my super-organized closet the once-over, and wondered how long it would take me to make it my typical mess.

*Maybe I'll turn over a new leaf and keep it neat.* Then I thought again, *maybe I can at least make the pile on the floor closer to the closet doors.*

I slid a pair of pants off a hanger, and as I finished dressing, I started thinking about the conversation I had with my mom about Mitch. It really got me heated up when I thought about all he had to deal with. *Darn Mrs. Kennedy for messing everything up!*

Mitch arrived at seven. Walking to the car kind of reminded me of our first date, almost a year ago. I remembered being about to explode with nervousness and excitement. It was so much easier now.

Driving to pick up Davey Barr's girlfriend, I asked Davey about her, wondering if it was someone I knew from Northfield. When he told me her name was Jan DeStefano, the name sounded familiar. I thought I remembered her from summer league softball. I wondered if she had changed 'cause when she was twelve or thirteen she was a wild one. It seemed to me she had gotten thrown out of a game once for her mouth, and when we picked her up I recognized her.

She was that girl. But gone were her brown ponytail and freckles. Instead, her shaggy hair was dyed black with what looked like blue streaks. She wore a ton of makeup and had a ring in her brow. All I could see was how different she was than Tori. *What was Davey thinking?*

The entrance to the theater was packed and while the boys waited in line for tickets, Jan said to me, "So, Jackie, it's been a long time. You sure got a hot looking boyfriend there. You still into the sports thing?"

"Thanks, and yeah, I play hockey at school. How about you?" I asked, trying to be polite.

"Nah," she said. "I had enough of rules with those coaches and umpires when we used to play softball. Besides I've got a job working after school. Need the money for the good times, you know what I mean?"

"You mean drugs?" I asked. It was the first thing that came into my mind.

She looked surprised. "What made you say that?" she asked. "I'm not stupid! Just a few beers now and then, it costs money you know, especially when you need to bribe someone to get 'em for you." Then she narrowed her eyes and said, "You got some kind of problem with that?"

Talk about an awkward moment! The whole conversation had gotten out of hand and I didn't know what to say. Fortunately Mitch and Davey walked up to us with the tickets and I was saved from becoming more stupid than I already felt.

"All set?" Mitch asked, looking at me curiously.

I kind of half smiled at Jan, then looked at Mitch and said, "Sure." I took his hand and felt more than a little relieved to be walking into the dark theater.

Watching the movie, a chick flick, *thank you very much guys,* my thoughts turned back to Jan. I was feeling guilty jumping to my conclusion about drugs. I know it was because of how she looked. I wondered about her question. It seemed like some sort of challenge. I knew some kids drank at parties and other things, too, but not people I hung around with. Did that mean I couldn't be friendly with people that did drink? I didn't know. I wished Matt wasn't gone. He would have known what I should have said and the right thing to do.

Mitch leaned over and whispered, "You like the movie? You seem kind of far away."

"Sorry. The movie is great. I was just thinking."

"Don't work too hard there, we're supposed to be having fun," he said, gently tugging at one of my curls.

After the movie Jan and I stopped in the restroom. As I was drying my hands, Jan was looking in the mirror putting on a whole new face from top to bottom.

"How long does it take you to do that?" I asked, wondering how she could ever make it to school on time.

She turned around to face me. "Long enough to keep my mom on edge," she said. I must have looked perplexed 'cause then she said, "Do you have a mom who wants you to be one kind of person and you know it's not you, so you work harder to do your own thing?"

I nodded my head in agreement. I totally got what she meant.

"Well, my mom always had it in her head that I should be a nun," she said.

I couldn't help it. I laughed right out loud, and then quickly covered my mouth.

"See, not me, right?" she said. "So I do the makeup thing and twist the rules a little bit just to make sure she knows I have no intention of heading in that direction."

Then I told Jan about me and my mom and how she **so** didn't understand my love of sports.

Later that evening as Major Kennedy stopped to let off Jan, she leaned up from the back seat and said, "Good to see you, Jackie. Take care of yourself, okay?"

I turned around to say goodbye knowing she was waiting to see how I was going to end things. Like, if it was all good, or maybe those few moments in the ladies room didn't matter and now I was going to blow her off with some phony politeness or something.

"It's been a long time, I'm glad we saw each other again, too," I said, and I made sure my words reached my eyes because in my gut I meant it. It **had** been a good night.

As Jan walked away, instinct told me I passed the 'Jan test.' Maybe I wasn't her version of cool, but I discovered we had more in common than I thought.

"I'm going to miss you like crazy when I'm away," Mitch said quietly as he walked me to my front door.

"Me too. But I think Mrs. Fortunato will keep me plenty busy."

He gave a little smile and said, "I'm sure."

When we got to our front porch, Mitch pulled me into his arms and started to kiss me like usual – soft and dreamy. Then he took me by surprise and the kiss kicked up a notch, and emotions that Mitch normally kept in check came spilling out all over the place. Abruptly he stopped and mumbled, "Love you, Jackie." Then he turned and walked away quickly to the car.

As I watched them drive off my knees felt like rubber. After a moment I let myself in the house and called out, "I'm back."

Upstairs, I closed my bedroom door and flopped onto the bed. My head was spinning with feelings that were all jumbled up. I didn't realize 'til that moment how important it was to have my own space. I don't think I could have taken any of Lizzie's third grade chatter right then.

I looked down at my copper bracelet and turned it around on my wrist. It was feeling tight like it had a hold of me instead of being just a pretty reminder of Mitch. I couldn't understand why I thought that.

*Were Mitch and I getting too serious? Mitch said he loved me, at least I think that's what he said. I should feel thrilled but, ... I don't ... I feel ... I don't want to think about what I feel.*

Between my conversations with Jan, my brother's 'don't grow up too fast,' and the intensity of Mitch's goodbye, it took me a long time to get to sleep.

That night I dreamed I was walking down the aisle as a bride, but I wasn't in a white dress. Instead, I was wearing my ninth grade hockey uniform. When the minister asked me to say 'I do,' I told him maybe I do, but maybe I don't. I was just too young to know what was right, and anyhow lots of people get divorced, and I was late for my game. In my dream I turned to Mitch to see if he understood, but all of a sudden he disappeared, and then I woke up.

I looked at the clock. It was three A.M. and I couldn't get back to sleep. I slipped out of bed and crossed the hall to my old room.

# - 13 -

I awoke in my old twin bed and could feel the impact of my restless night's sleep. Every part of my body felt like it was tied up in knots. *I'm so glad I'm going to the Hanson's today. It's just the break I need.*

I rolled over to find Lizzie quietly taping her art work all over the walls. She sure wasn't wasting any time making the room her own.

"Hey, Lizzie, it looks great."

She turned and looked at me as if she wasn't sure she was doing the right thing. "Is this okay?" she asked.

"Sure, the room's yours now."

She grinned, dropped her drawings, and came over to sit on the edge of the bed. She hesitated for a moment, then hugged me and said, "I missed you last night when I went to sleep."

I was glad she didn't ask why she found me in her room when she awoke. I don't think I could have explained it if I tried. I leaned up on one elbow and surveyed the room. "I know you're going to love this room," I said. "And, sometime soon Mom and Dad will let you have a friend over and you'll have the best time giggling all night long." For a moment I flashed to when the twins and I had done that very thing. Life was so easy then. I just hadn't realized it. I smoothed out my sister's hair and took her hand to go downstairs feeling just a little envious of how simple her life must feel.

\*        \*        \*

That afternoon I decided to ride my bike over to the Hanson's rather than have my parents drive me. It felt good. No thinking, just letting the breeze hit my face. I was parking my bike by the Hanson's garage when Jules came out the back door carrying a cooler.

"Hey, just in time, I need some help with the ice," she said.

After we filled the cooler with ice and sodas, she asked, "How about a game of HORSE?"

"Okay, you go first," I said grinning. I was **so** not a basketball player. I could dribble well enough, but the shooting department was definitely questionable.

Jules grabbed a basketball out of the garage and the two of us headed to the basketball court that her dad had built at the back of their driveway. It had a key painted on the blacktop and everything. Real serious stuff! As we traded turns shooting, we started talking about hockey.

"So do you think I'm out of line wanting to make varsity?" she asked, tossing me the ball.

I dribbled the ball in place, thinking about the next shot, then drove to the basket. I got my own rebound and turned to face her.

"No, you're not out of line," I said. "You could be one of the top defenders from what I've seen so far. Maybe there are two others and Mandy, of course, but that's it."

"So you **have** been checking people out," she said.

"What do you mean?"

"You know what I mean, sizing up the competition," she said. "There's nothing wrong with that. Did you think there was?"

"I guess not," I said, and studied the writing on the ball for a moment like it was magic and would give me a better answer. Finally I passed Jules the ball.

"Jackie, we both could make it. Maybe not start right away, but definitely we could be players that Coach would have to think about. I can't believe you don't want that." She dribbled in place, then paused and said, "What's stopping you? Our friends?"

I didn't say anything.

"Look, maybe some of them will make it, too," she said, "and maybe not. Some don't care. Look at Tori. She's a really good athlete. She's just not hungry for it and admits it. But you're different. Its part of you, I know it. You need to follow what's inside of you, Jackie, and not worry about the others." She started to dribble again and said, "Think about it."

I watched Jules drive toward the basket and pull up short for a ten foot jumper. She was so confident. I put my hands on my hips and looked down at the ground. *Why couldn't I be more like her?*

"Hey," a familiar voice called from behind me, "are you going to let her get away with an easy shot like that?"

I looked over my shoulder and grinned at Chris Hanson, the twins' brother. He was a senior at St. Benedict's Prep and a star on the school's basketball team.

"Hey, Chris, what's up?"

I'd known Chris forever, since he was like twelve or thirteen. To me, being around him was like having another older brother, someone you could kid around with. Of course, most girls didn't think like that. They followed him around like puppies and I got it, 'cause he could be in the movies with that face of his. His bright blue eyes were insane, and his smile, when it came your way, was a killer.

There was a lot more to him, too, once you got past the gorgeous part. Even though he was quiet, there was something about him, like he would always have your back; that made me like him. Plus, he sure put up with a lot, what with all the idiotic stunts his sisters and I had pulled over the years.

He was eyeing the basket, probably figuring how he could snuff out Jules and me with his three-pointers, when he said, "If Princess Tori ever finishes dressing any time soon, how about a little two on two?"

"Okay, Jules and I will take on you and Tori."

"Deal, but no dunking, Jackie," he said teasingly.

I let out a long breath. It felt like someone had just rung the bell for recess and suddenly the day seemed a little brighter.

After dinner, Chris was leaning against the kitchen counter while his mom and I were putting away the leftovers. I noticed it was getting dark out and said I should be going.

"Let Chris take you," Mrs. Hanson said. "He can put your bike on the back of his car."

"Oh, he doesn't have to do that. I'll be all right."

"Don't you believe I can get you home safely?" he asked. He pushed away from the counter and started to reach into his pocket. "I'll show you the score on my driving test if you want."

"If a student from St. Benedict's can get a license, it looks like I'll have no problem getting mine someday," I said with a grin.

"Ouch, you're tough! Come on, let's get your bike."

Making the fifteen minute drive to my house, Chris and I got caught up on life. He was so easy to talk to, and before I knew it I was home. He lifted my bike off the rack on the back of his car like it was a kid's tricycle. I think he only used one hand. Jeez, he was big. Between him and Mitch I wondered if there was something in the South Jersey water supply and wondered how come it hadn't worked on me.

"You don't drive too badly. I guess the roads are still safe," I said, as he walked my bike to the garage.

He grinned and wished me luck with hockey. Then he told me to be careful and to try not to knock anyone over.

"Very funny," I said, grinning, and waved a thanks as he got into his car.

*     *     *

Getting ready for bed I thought about the conversation I had with Jules. I felt stuck. If I did make varsity I would definitely miss my friends. And if I played with the upper-classmen, I would need a rearview mirror to watch for someone sneaking up on me, trying to stab me in the back. It was another night of thinking too much and school hadn't even started yet! I needed to sleep. Morning was coming fast enough.

# - 14 -

My dad was alone in the kitchen enjoying the morning's sports page. While I was making toast, I asked, "Dad, when did Matt first make varsity? I forget."

My dad lowered the paper and thought for a moment. "Hmmm, I guess he became a starter somewhere in the middle of his sophomore year. He might have played only a little in the beginning, but gradually the coach played him more and more."

"How did he like playing with the varsity?"

Dad put down the paper and studied me over his mug of coffee. He took a sip and then he said, "He was thrilled."

I interrupted, "But what about the other players?"

"What about them? Why are you asking?" By now my dad had forgotten the sports page and his breakfast, so I kept going.

"Well, was Matt the only sophomore to play?"

"He might have been. Jackie, you need to know something. Playing on a team is just like being in class. Some people just make quicker progress than others. Remember when you first started reading and some kids picked it up fast and then others took longer?"

I nodded. I thought I might have been in the 'longer' group. I sat down opposite my dad and began curling up the edges of a napkin trying to process everything.

"If you think he was waiting for someone to catch up to him, you don't know your brother," Dad said. "Everyone wanted it. Maybe some people were jealous at first, but I doubt it lasted."

I understood what Dad was saying, but that was guys and I wasn't sure things were the same for girls.

My dad walked over to the coffee maker and poured himself another cup. He turned to me and asked, "What's this about? Do you think you have a chance to play varsity?"

I shrugged my shoulders. "I don't know, probably not. Jules and I were talking about it, that's all. I like playing with my friends, and well, some people might get mad."

"Jackie, anyone who gives you any grief for making varsity is not your friend."

*     *     *

Waiting on the front steps for my ride with Mrs. Hanson, I tossed the whole conversation around in my head. Actually I should say conversations – the one with my dad and the one with myself that I hadn't shared with anyone, the one about me and the upperclassmen. My dad hadn't really understood what had concerned me the most. I took a couple of deep breaths and then made up my mind, and when I got in the car I said to Jules, "I think for now I just better focus on making the team."

Tori turned around in the front seat. She looked surprised. I guess she and Jules had talked. I checked Jules out of the corner of my eye. She was ignoring me, and then she turned her head to stare out the window.

When we got to school, even though Jules wasn't happy about it, I felt much more settled about what I should be going for – just learn as much hockey as I could and keep my distance from the older girls.

\* \* \*

On Wednesday, Mrs. Fortunato announced that her decisions on cuts would be posted after practice. I sensed everyone's heartbeat quicken. It reminded me of freshman year when I thought I would hyperventilate hurrying down the hall to the gym to find out if I made the team. Seeing my name on that team list was one of the best moments ever.

This year I felt a little better about myself and thought I had a pretty good chance to at least make JV. As we started our drills I paid more attention to the other forwards. There were Bri and Kat, the seniors from camp, five juniors who hadn't attended camp, and then the sophomores, Sam Jones, Sarah Graff, Steph Jankowski, and myself. I wondered which forwards would get cut and who would make the varsity and JV teams.

After practice we rushed over to see the list. My confidence faltered for a minute and it crept into my mind that maybe I got it all wrong, that I wasn't good enough to make it. I saw a few upperclassmen check the list then hurry to their cars with their heads down. Tori pushed her way through the crowd and looked over the head of the girl in front of her. After a moment she turned to Jules and me and gave us a 'thumbs up.' I let out a long sigh of relief and moved away so others could check for their own names. Now that we made the team, the real work was going to start for all of us.

\*       \*       \*

The next day Mrs. Fortunato met us on the field and told us to sit in the bleachers. I wondered what was up. She usually ran us to death first thing. I thought it would be great if she gave us a day off from the sprints 'cause my legs felt like they were stuck in cement.

She congratulated us on making the team, gave us our game schedules, and then she handed out some paper and pencils. Looking on the paper I saw a list of questions and felt like I was in school already. Ugh! Then we were asked to write all this stuff, like our personal goals, how we could help the team, and what we needed to work on. My mind was spinning. I was **so** not ready to do any thinking.

There were two problems answering this stuff. First, if I was too honest, would Mrs. Fortunato think I was weak? But if I censored how I felt, was I really being honest with my coach?

I sighed and looked at the others busy writing. I looked up and watched Mrs. Fortunato busy organizing the equipment. I knew I had to make a decision.

Before long Mrs. Fortunato called out, "One minute." Everybody groaned and started writing faster. My hand started cramping up from all the writing and I thought maybe next summer Coach should include some finger exercises in our workout program.

The papers were collected and Mrs. Fortunato told us we needed to sign up for meetings she would be having over the next two days. The twins and I made our appointments close together on Friday so we could kind of have each others' backs if things didn't go well.

*  *  *

After Friday's practice we grilled the other sophomores about how their meetings went, and most of them said that she just went over stuff on their sheets. Walking toward the girls' physical education office, Tori said, "I don't want to do this. Can't we skip it?"

Jules laughed at her, "Stop being so dramatic. She's not going to take your head off. You haven't played that many days to screw up."

Tori jumped on her. "Okay, 'Ms. I have it all together.' Let's see how your meeting goes."

Tori's meeting took just ten minutes, and she came out smiling. "Cake," she said to Jules and me.

"Good luck," Jules said to me when she came out fifteen minutes later.

Mrs. Fortunato looked up from her desk, "Jackie, come in and take a seat. How was your summer?"

Waiting for my answer, she got up and shut the door behind me. My heart wanted to jump out of my chest. *Big bad woman, big mad woman!* The comment haunted me. I felt like I was in some torture chamber and maybe there was truth serum hidden in a drawer.

"Jackie?"

I took a deep breath and started to answer the question, but Mrs. Fortunato interrupted me, smiling. "Jackie, this is not a torture chamber and you should know by now that I don't bite."

*Jeez, is she a mind reader, too?*

She caught my eye and laughed. "Okay, maybe I do bark a little."

I grinned at her comment ... *this is going to be okay.* I finally opened my mouth, "It was a good summer and I had fun at camp."

"That's great," she replied, then turning back to the papers on her desk, she said, "I went over the sheet you filled out and I'm sure we can work on some of the skills you want to improve upon. There are a couple of things I'd like to talk about right now, though."

*Uh-oh,* I thought, and I sat up straighter.

"First off, I think you are a first-rate worker, and I wish more players had your dedication," she said.

*Wow!*

She went on, "I am a little curious about the confidence issue you wrote about, though."

"Well," and this was hard to talk about especially to her, but I said, "Sometimes I don't think I do a good enough job."

"Does somebody tell you that?" she asked.

"No, I just think it, I guess."

She sat back in her chair for a moment, seeming to be debating something in her mind, then she said, "Don't repeat this to anyone, but you remind me of myself when I was your age."

I thought I'd slide to the floor when she said that and gripped the sides of the chair so I wouldn't look goofy reaching up to pinch myself to check if I was dreaming.

Mrs. Fortunato looked off in the distance for a moment and I wondered what she was thinking. Finally she said, "I demanded a lot of myself when I was young. I really wanted to be good. When things did not come easy enough, or if I made a lot mistakes, I worried over it too much. Does that sound familiar?"

"Yes." I thought my eyes would pop out of my head with surprise. *My coach thinks I remind her of when she was young. This is mad crazy!*

"I think you have wonderful potential as an individual player, of course, but as a team leader someday, too. So I'm going to ask you to do two things for me this year, okay?"

"Okay," I said, and right then I thought I would have 'okayed' just about anything she asked me to do.

She said she wanted me to keep a journal and then she handed me a small notebook. I was to write down two goals for myself every three weeks in the notebook, and every day I was to keep track of how well I was moving toward those goals. The second thing she wanted me to do was have a secret buddy, someone on the team that I was supposed to help during the season. But I couldn't tell the person I was her helper.

"So, any questions?" she asked finally.

"No," but I was thinking, *well yeah, about a million.*

"It's been good to see you again, Jackie. I'm certainly looking forward to having you with the team this year. She looked down at her clipboard, "If you will, please send in Stephanie Jankowski."

I found the twins waiting for me by the parking lot. Tori was stretched out on the grass catching the last tanning rays of summer while Jules was pacing back and forth.

"So," Tori asked, "how was it? She kept you in there long enough." Then she spied the notebook. "What's that?"

"Oh, it's kind of like homework," I said. "She wants me to write stuff down every day. What did she say to you, Jules?"

"She liked how I was playing defense so far. She said if I keep working hard I might get some playing time with the varsity. Did she tell you the same thing?"

"No."

Tori stood up and put her arm around my shoulder. "Maybe you have to do your homework first before she'll even give you a uniform," she said, and gave me a playful shove.

As I got in the car I thought that maybe Tori had something. Maybe having a notebook was like repeating a grade or like doing extra work to catch up. I leaned my head against the seat, closed my eyes, and felt the excitement from the meeting disappear.

*     *     *

That night I leafed through the blank journal, thinking about goals and who I needed to pick for my secret buddy. My cell phone rang. It was Mitch asking me how things were going.

"Okay," I said to his question. "I'm just sitting here trying to figure out what to write in a journal Mrs. Fortunato gave me."

"What? Like a diary?"

"I guess, except she gets to read it."

"Uh-oh, I guess no boyfriend stuff, like your heart beats only for me."

I laughed. "Don't be silly, it's about hockey. So ... did you catch any big ones?"

"I caught our supper last night, skinned it and all. It's really nice up here in the mountains. You can see an amazing amount of stars. It would be better here if you were sitting right beside me, though."

"That sounds a lot better than doing all the running we're doing," I said.

"My dad has worked it out that we can stay until Monday," he said. "I just wanted to call and say hi."

After we said our good-byes, I tried to imagine myself sitting in front of a campfire, my head resting on Mitch's shoulder. It seemed very romantic and nothing like the 'you're getting too serious' stuff that Matt had been talking about. Glancing at the clock, I saw it was getting late. Jotting down two goals for my journal I picked Ellen to be the person I would try to help out. She'd be behind for sure once she came back to hockey, so maybe wouldn't mind my help.

I turned off the light and rolled over onto my side. I was good to go, I thought. Maybe playing hockey this year wouldn't be as complicated as I thought.

# - 15 -

On Saturday, the whole McKendry clan was going to Matt's college to see his soccer scrimmage. We knew he probably wouldn't be playing. He had already called and warned us not to expect it. I asked my mom if I could invite the twins, but Tori was busy, so it was just Jules. We picked her up around noon.

"Thank goodness practice was short," Jules said as she hopped into the backseat with Lizzie and me.

"Yeah, all she did was run us to death for two hours," I laughed.

"How come you had to talk with her afterwards?"

"She wanted to go over my notebook stuff."

Jules kind of gave me a look, seemed to change her mind, and turned to Lizzie and asked, "So how is the biggest flirt at Washington Elementary? You got a boyfriend or two yet?"

"No," Lizzie answered smugly, "I'm too young. You have to wait 'til fifth grade, silly."

Jules broke up laughing and Mom turned in her seat, "Julianna Hanson, don't you give that child any ideas. She has enough of her own, thank you very much." Then she laughed.

I looked into the rearview mirror and saw even Dad's eyes crinkle at that one.

"I'm sorry your sister couldn't come," Mom said.

"She was too, but she still has to go through all the boys in Northfield before she's ready to scout out the college scene."

My mom looked like she was going to say something, but Jules beat her to it.

"Just kidding, Mrs. McKendry, but she does have a date later and her art class was today, too."

I thought about Tori and all of her 'male' conquests. She sure didn't let any grass grow under her feet. I wondered about Jules, she had shown no interest in anyone. Did that mean she found all the boys boring or that the boys we knew were intimidated by her? It was hard to figure out. Jules was just as good-looking as her sister, but she wasn't flirty like Tori. I figured, if it wasn't for Mitch I wouldn't have anyone special in my life either, so maybe I was just lucky.

*　　*　　*

Once we arrived at the college we had no trouble finding the soccer complex. It wasn't as big as a football stadium or anything, but it was gated and had really nice bleachers. It even had its own snack bar which was always a plus for me.

Mom and Dad wanted to watch the pre-game warm up and told us we had some time until the game started. Jules and I decided we wanted to see what the rest of the athletic facilities were like so we took off toward the field house.

When we entered the building we were surprised at its large foyer. It was super impressive with its walls of photos and plaques dedicated to the college's All-Americans and national champions.

"Hey Jackie," Jules said, "come here."

Among all of the football, soccer, and baseball awards and trophies, Jules had found a large plaque with a picture of a female field hockey player on it. Looking closely at the plaque we saw the player's honors. "Wow, a two-time All-American," Jules said. "Look at all the goals she scored, Jackie."

Walking a few feet further away, I said, "Look, Jules, here's another one."

Jules walked over to see what I was reading, "Cathy Leighty, class of ... hey she's still here, she's a senior. And look," she said reading her bio, "she's from Toms River."

We laughed and high-fived each other 'cause the girl's high school was just an hour away from ours which made us all like neighbors. Our fifteen-year-old thinking was that all girls from New Jersey were bound to be great hockey players. I mean I knew it wasn't true 'cause I remembered the girls from camp. Still, it was fun to think that way for a minute.

We continued walking down the hall and it was then we heard girls' voices and the unmistakable stop and hit sounds of hockey balls. We glanced at each other and simultaneously knew we had to check it out.

At the end of the hallway we peeked into the open doorway of a gym where an indoor practice was going on. "It must be the college's team," I said. I looked at my watch. "We have ten minutes. Want to stay and watch?"

"Do fish swim?"

We stood by the door, so no one would notice us, and were blown away by what we saw. We'd never seen hockey played with such speed and accuracy. Jules whispered, "See the girl with dark hair in the green tank top? I think that's her, the All-American in the picture."

My eyes followed every move the girl made. She was in constant motion, even when she wasn't near the ball. I thought she was magic.

After a few minutes, I checked my watch. "We better go Jules, or my parents will have a fit."

Leaving the building we broke into a trot. "I want to be able to play that way someday," Jules said.

"Me too. That was unbelievable. Did you see how much that girl moved? She made me tired just looking at her. I don't even know why she was moving."

"I think she was trying to make space."

"What?"

"You know, if you move, the defender has to move, too. That leaves a space to put the ball."

"Oh yeah, right," I said, but she might as well have given me her explanation in some foreign language for all the good it did me.

\*     \*     \*

"Where were you two? We were getting worried," Mom said, as we made our way up the bleachers.

"Mom, you won't believe what we saw. The hockey team was practicing inside. They were awesome."

Mom gave me a blank stare, and said, "That's nice, dear," and turned her attention back to the field. She **so** did not get my interest in hockey.

The soccer scrimmage was a pretty good one I guess, though I was still thinking more about the hockey we had just seen. Toward the end of the second half, I saw both coaches making some substitutions. Matt got up and started jogging behind the benches.

"Mom, I think Matt's going in," I said.

"Yes, dear, it's exciting."

I was so used to my brother being such a star on the field that once he was in the game it kind of surprised me that he wasn't doing any better than anybody else on his team. If he wasn't my brother I don't think I would even notice him.

*Is college really all that different?*

Suddenly there was an interception, and a long counter pass down the field. Matt took off. Now I could see the speed he still had over most of the others. He dodged one player and was able to get a strong shot off into the corner of the cage. At the last minute the goalie got his hands on the ball and tipped it over the cage.

"Aw," I said, "he didn't score."

Dad turned to me, "Good shot, though. The goalie just had a terrific save. Your brother just needs to get confident out there."

On the corner kick the ball curled in toward the cage and Matt jumped up to head it in and again the goalie came up with a spectacular save.

"Now we're rolling," Jules said. "Go Matt," she yelled.

As the game ended, my dad turned to my mom and said, "That was pretty good, Anne. He got in for twelve minutes. More than he thought."

I guessed that was good. I mean, I'd only seen Matt as the go-to guy. This was like starting all over, and I guessed that could be the same way for Jules and me someday, or at least me.

*     *     *

After the game we waited on the field house steps for Matt and his roommate to change. Just as they were coming out we saw some girls leaving the building too.

*They must be the hockey players. Boy, they're a lot bigger close up. Maybe I'm too little to play in college.* Suddenly coming from Jersey didn't seem to be much of a help into turning me into a good player someday and I figured I better work extra hard.

As I turned back to my brother, Matt introduced his roommate, Cooker Hayes, to everyone. Matt explained to us that the team called Cooker 'the enforcer.'

"What's that mean?" I asked.

"That's what Dad was," said Matt with a grin. "An enforcer makes sure the other team has a tough time penetrating the goal area, and if they do, he makes them pay, and bruises them up a little bit."

"But he looks so nice," Mom said, amazed that Cooker could act 'so animal' on the field, and the boys broke out laughing.

When we all started walking to the parking lot I overheard my brother say, "Mom, didn't you ever see Dad play?"

"My playing days were done when I met your mother," Dad said. "If she had seen me play she probably wouldn't have dated me."

I saw a twinkle in my dad's eyes. *So there's more to the story than "we met in college." I want to hear more.*

"So how exactly did you guys meet?" I asked.

"Oh, I don't think Cooker wants to hear that old stuff. We'll save it for another time," Mom said, seeming embarrassed.

*Uh-oh, I think I've hit on a juicy story. I'm going to definitely get it out of one of you someday, Mom.*

\*     \*     \*

We all went out to dinner and afterwards we visited my brother's dorm. I was shocked by how small the room was. Of course, I'd stayed in a college dorm for hockey camp, but we hadn't been trying to fill it with everything we owned. At least Lindsay hadn't.

"Where are all the closets for your winter clothes?" I asked.

Cooker chuckled. "They did away with our walk-in closet and made it into a single for the RA," he said.

Matt saw my confusion. "An RA is a resident assistant. They help out the people who live in the dorm and they get their own room pretty much for free."

Cooker nudged my brother and Matt began to crack his knuckles. Something was up.

"Uh, Dad, the rest of the freshmen reported to campus today," Matt said finally. "Tonight the school is hosting a welcome party for all the freshmen and ..." He paused, hoping that Dad would get the hint.

My dad laughed. "I guess that's our clue to leave," he said, then put his arm around my mom drawing her to the door. "Have fun tonight fellows," he said, and we quickly said good-bye.

It was quiet riding home. It seemed like our college visit had spun everyone into their own little world. I wondered if my brother missed us half as much as we missed him. Probably not, I thought, as he seemed so excited about everything. All he could talk about at dinner was his new coach and the other guys on the team. It was like he was making a whole new family for himself at the college. I looked at my parents, and Lizzie, fast asleep with her head in Jules' lap. *Even though it might be cool to play college hockey, especially if I could be as good as the girl in green, this is my family, even Jules.* Imagining there might be another one waiting for me someday was pretty hard to wrap my head around.

*    *    *

The next few days passed quickly, and by Tuesday we were getting ready for our first scrimmage. It was exciting warming up on the varsity field. The older players were pretty much ignoring us and going about their business, which was a good thing. But I have to be honest, even though I was sure it wouldn't happen, it still seemed strange when the varsity line-up was read and I didn't hear my name. I wondered if that's the way it had been for Matt at his first college scrimmage.

Standing on the sidelines when the opening whistle blew definitely felt like being in no man's land. *Where **did** I belong?* I had been so positive that being with the JV was what I really wanted. Watching the action from the bench area, I wasn't so sure.

While our varsity dominated the other team, it didn't appear to be the threatening unit like last year's varsity. I turned to Lindsay, "What do you think?"

"They're doing okay, I guess."

"Hey Jackie," Tori yelled over to me, "Coach just called for you. Hurry up."

I was startled at first, and then quickly ran over to Mrs. Fortunato.

"I want you to go in for Bri," Mrs. Fortunato said with her eyes still on the field.

"Now?" I asked, stupidly.

Mrs. Fortunato turned and looked at me kind of funny and said, "Yes, now would be a good time, but I think you need a stick and mouth guard."

I felt the heat in my cheeks, embarrassed that I didn't know enough to have my stuff with me. I ran over to the bench, grabbed my things, and reported to the scorers' table, telling them who I was going in for. I sure wished it hadn't been for Bri. Waiting for her to come out I started to give her a 'good job' fist bump 'cause that's just what we usually did to keep spirits up, but she moved past me pretending she didn't see me and went straight to the bench. I never felt so unwelcome and alone as I jogged out to take my position on the field.

In the ten minutes Mrs. Fortunato had me in the scrimmage I think I touched the ball once. It seemed like the older girls were pretending I wasn't on the field, but maybe I was just being sensitive. Finally Mandy stole the ball, looked up, and yelled to me, "Go."

I took off down the field just 'cause she said to. And then she sent me this great pass. I caught it on the dead run. I didn't even have to slow down it was that good. As I neared the striking circle, I caught Kat out of the corner of my eye and passed her the ball.

That was really about it, the extent of my time with the varsity, 'cause Mrs. Fortunato didn't play me in the second half. Jules got in for about fifteen minutes, though, and I thought she did great. After the varsity game there was an extra playing period, almost like a mini JV game, and Jules and I got to play with our friends again. It seemed just like the end of last year, everything easy and comfortable.

"You did great out there with the varsity," I told Jules when we were riding home.

"It felt pretty good," she said. "All the other defenders talked to me a lot and that helped. How about you?"

"I don't know. I didn't get the ball much."

"Can't help you there, Jackie," she said.

At the next morning's practice Ms. Gillespie kept me with the JV, but Jules moved back and forth between the two groups. Then, in the last ten minutes, Mrs. Fortunato switched things up and changed all the forwards around so I was playing with the varsity defenders. Even when I thought I was open, nobody sent the ball my way. It was like I was invisible. It made me feel stupid even being on the field. I didn't know if I was doing something wrong or if they just didn't like me. I mean what was so good about being with a varsity team if nobody wanted you and didn't pass you the ball?

# - 16 -

When I was a freshman, I had been in a state of clueless panic as I got ready for my very first day of high school. I had felt like one of those old-time sailors who were leaving home to explore unknown lands, all the while wondering if any minute I might fall off the edge of the world instead.

This year was so different. I was excited, of course, but in a good way. I was armed with my maps and compass. Homeroom – known, class schedule – charted, and the ultimate destination, the hockey field with my friends, – already clearly marked with hazards hopefully averted. The only thing missing was the morning rides in my brother's car. I didn't realize how much getting chauffeured to school had spoiled me 'til I climbed back onto the old yellow bus and sat in those uncomfortable seats.

Sliding into a seat in the back of homeroom, I hadn't even dropped my knapsack on the floor when Jules walked in the door. Soon we were joined by Ellen, who was still walking with a big-time limp. Just as the late bell rang, I looked up from my chatting with the girls to see Mitch's friends, Kurt Evans and Will Stanley, hurry into the room. They spotted us in the back and waved before taking the few remaining seats.

Kurt immediately went into entertainment mode, sharing his latest jokes with those around him, while Will opened up a paperback book and start reading. It struck me that Will might be the literary type, and therefore, a good match for Jules who always got straight A's. I wondered why I had just thought of it and decided I'd have to talk to Mitch and see if we could make things happen.

Later, walking into my fourth period gym class, there was chaos everywhere. For a moment I felt off balance, like it was freshman year all over again. It didn't take long for me to recover, though, knowing that all the insanity would disappear as soon as we were divided up and met our assigned teachers.

I gazed around the room and found a familiar face. It was a face that made me smile all over. Mitch was sitting on the top row of the bleachers with Kurt and Will. I waved up to him, found Jules, and together we climbed the bleachers to sit with the boys. A few minutes later Lindsay joined us. From where we sat, watching the rest of the students filing in, we were like Kings of the Hill, like we had life all figured out, and nothing could get in our way.

All six of us were assigned to Mr. Rose's class. He announced that our first activity would be flag football. I made a face 'cause I thought I was going to get chewed up, but Mitch laughed, slid his arm around me in a way that the teacher wouldn't notice.

"Don't worry, I'll protect you," he said.

"Yeah, Mitch, but who is going to protect the rest of us from Jackie," Kurt Evans said, and laughed.

The boys thought it was real funny, but Jules just smiled. She understood me the best and knew that even though I was little, if I was really pushed, I could come out smoking.

*     *     *

Since the gym was at the other end of the building, by the time I reached the cafeteria it was already packed. I spotted Tori toward the back of the room with her tray of food, still searching for an open table. After a few minutes I joined her, and we eventually discovered a few empty seats at a half-filled table with three boys already there.

"Do you mind if we sit here for today?" Tori asked one of the boys.

"No, its okay," he said, and immediately turned back to his friends.

Once our initial food attack was over, we surveyed the room to see if we knew anybody. The place seemed filled to capacity. Some kids were even standing. We decided finding our own table tomorrow might be tough. A few minutes later Ellen came hobbling over.

"It took me forever to get here, she said. She looked around, "This place is a zoo. I can't believe I even found you guys."

"How's the leg?" Tori asked.

"I'm off the crutches obviously, but I've got a ways to go." She tossed her backpack on the ground and collapsed into her seat. "I miss hockey so much," she said. "Thank goodness Mrs. Fortunato took into account that I was injured and kept me with the team. What's been going on?"

Before we could answer her one of the boys turned in his seat and asked, "What, are you guys jocks or something?"

"What's it to you?" Tori asked, getting a little huffy thinking maybe he was going to give us a hard time.

The boy had on faded jeans and a torn black T-shirt from some band I never heard of. His brown shaggy hair flopped over eyes that crinkled up at the edges when he heard Tori's comment.

"Chill baby, I meant no disrespect," he said, and put his hands up in the air as a sign of mock surrender.

Tori did a double take. I'd seen this look before. His offhanded attitude intrigued her, I could tell. *Hmmm, he could be her next heartbreak victim.* All of a sudden I thought lunch period could get very interesting.

The bell rang and Ellen, Tori, and I made our way to the exit together. Unfortunately we were all going in different directions. Shortly I found myself walking next to the brown-haired guy from our lunch table. He looked at me and said, "So, Reds, where you heading?"

"Only my boyfriend calls me that. It's Jackie to you," I said.

"Excuse me," he exclaimed, drawing out the words like I had really offended him or something. I gave him my 'don't mess with me' look, but it probably needed some work since he definitely was not put off.

He smiled and said, "I'm James."

I studied him out of the corner of my eye. I noticed a stud in his ear and a small tattoo on his neck and wondered if it was real.

Seeing my English room up ahead I was saved from saying anything more. I turned into the room, but this James was right behind me. I quickly took a seat in the first row. Thank goodness he didn't follow me. Instead, he strolled over to a seat by the window and flopped down.

Mr. Barrows, my teacher from freshman year, was leaning against the front wall, waiting for us to settle down. I was psyched to have him again. He had to be the reason for me being in Honors English this year. I was sure no teacher had ever recommended me for anything before, unless it was gym stuff of course.

Mr. Barrows took roll, then perched on top of his desk like he was ready to tell us a good story. This was one of the things I liked about him. It was as if our time together was special to him, and he made school about as much fun as school could ever be.

He told us we were going to be reading a lot of literature this year and discover what made good writing. I hoped the books were good ones 'cause I didn't like to read all that much.

He stood up. This was a signal that something important was going to be said, and he told us about our first assignment. We were going to have to write about something that occurred to us recently, something that we did not share with anyone else, and we had to do it in a hundred words or less.

I was stumped. I had never been too good about expressing my inner thoughts. This assignment could be a struggle. He told us we had two weeks to think about it and write it. Then he said that everyone in the class would read it.

*Ouch!* I didn't like that part at all, but Mr. Barrows went on and said our identity would be protected because he was going to use a number on the paper, not our name, thank goodness.

When the class ended and I was walking toward the front of the room, Mr. Barrows said, "I'm glad to have you in my class again, Jackie. You made a lot of progress last year."

"Thanks," I said, and smiled. Walking to my last class I thought about Mr. Barrows' faith in me and wondered why I couldn't believe in me as much as he did.

*     *     *

Hockey practices started to have a pattern. Most of the time I stayed with the other sophomores and would forget the older girls were around. Then I would get in a groove. If Mrs. Fortunato noticed me doing well she would pop me into the varsity lineup for a few minutes and I'd immediately freeze. Then she'd pull me out and send me back with the JV. I felt like a yo-yo. *Why didn't she just leave me alone?*

Toward the end of one practice she had me scrimmaging with the varsity again and it was just like all the other times. Feeling invisible, with no one passing me the ball, I was having a real pity party.

When I was subbed out, I went over to the end of the bench and sat down by myself. Leaning on my elbows, I twirled my stick in my hands hoping it could help me sort out what was going on in my head.

After a few minutes someone came over and sat down beside me. I looked up and saw it was Mandy Stevenson.

"What's going on?" she asked.

"I don't know," I said, shrugging my shoulders, trying to act cool. I sure didn't want to whine to a senior, especially the captain. That would make everyone think I was a big baby for sure, and not someone who could be playing varsity some day.

"Can I give you a suggestion?" she asked.

I nodded and stopped my twirling.

"I think you could get the ball more, but you're hiding," she said.

"Huh?"

"When you're playing against good defenders you can't just stand there. The defender will intercept the ball every time if she's any good. You've got to get her out of position. Make her move. Then there'll be space to pass the ball to you. You know?"

I gave Mandy a smile and nodded my head like I totally got what she was saying. When I checked my brain for light bulbs flashing, though, all I could see was a sign saying 'power outage.' Maybe I didn't want to play with the older girls, but I still wanted to be good. I was going to have to do some thinking about what she just told me.

*        *        *

That night I beat Mitch to it and called him. After we got caught up on our first day of school, I asked him how he got himself open in basketball. His answer made so much sense. I had been doing it all backwards. I had been waiting for the ball to be hit and then tried to chase after it, figuring I could just outrun my defender. I remembered the scrimmage when Mandy said 'go' before she hit the ball. I realized I had been open then, and just didn't know it.

Then I thought back to Jules explaining to me why that college hotshot was moving all over the place. It was to make the defenders change their position, just a little bit, so there could be a safe space to pass the ball. And just like that, everything fell into place. Mitch just pulled it all together for me and it completely changed how I looked at the game.

"Mitch, I get it. You're the best." I flopped back on my bed, so relieved I finally understood what I had to do.

"Glad to help," he said. "Say, Davey's brother is throwing a party next Saturday night. Davey is going to bring Jan, and he said we could come, too."

"Didn't his brother graduate a couple of years ago? Isn't everyone going to be lots older?"

"I guess, but maybe it would be fun to be around different people for a change. So what do you think?"

"I guess it'll be okay," I said. "I'll ask my dad tomorrow and see if he can drop me off at your house."

"Good deal. See you tomorrow."

*       *       *

In gym on Friday we had the best time. Our class was divided into two teams. Jules was quarterbacking our team, and I have to say she was pretty good. Mitch told me to just stand behind him and he'd block for me if I got the ball. Actually I was so busy laughing at all the friendly pushing and shoving going on around me it would have been kind of stupid of Jules to give me the ball. Right at the end, though, I took off downfield, and Jules, looking around, suddenly saw me open and hurled the ball as far as she could. I caught it and there were just two girls left to stop me. They grinned, gave me a little wave, and let me run by them. They probably didn't want to break a nail having to do anything physical was my thinking.

Once I crossed the goal line, I did a little victory dance, like you see on TV. Mitch ran in behind me, picked me up laughing, and swung me around. Right then my heart was just so full. I felt like the luckiest girl in the world. I thought it would last forever.

*       *       *

Saturday was the last scrimmage before the season opened. In the JV game, I tried to focus on making my defender move so I could get open. Sometimes I cut too early, but at least I was starting to get the idea. Once, I got myself open and was able to get my stick on a pass to deflect around the goalkeeper for a goal. It felt really good, like I was really on my way to understanding what I needed to do out there.

Jules didn't play JV with us, though. She played almost the whole varsity game. It felt kind of funny not being with her. As the twins and I were waiting for their mom to pick us up, I noticed that Tori was kind of quiet. She hadn't gotten into the varsity game either, and for the first time in her life had not been on the field with her sister. It seemed like hockey was splitting us up. Here I thought it was supposed to be something that would bring everyone together. Boy, was I naive.

# - 17 -

The next week flew by. Bri was acting all smug like she was some varsity star. It really irritated me, and when I watched her play I didn't get why she thought she was all that. I was pretty sure by next season I would be better than her, but for now, the more distance between us the better.

Friday was our opening game and the whole team decided to wear our white and blue uniform shirts to school. I checked my reflection in the bathroom mirror. The shirts were sleeveless and real lightweight, way better than our shirts from last year that had to have been at least a hundred years old. We were even given long-sleeved cold gear to wear under our shirts for when it was chilly out.

At lunch that day the boys at our table gave our uniform shirts the once-over and James grinned, "Uh-oh, big day for the jocks!" Tori glared at him and I chuckled to myself. I thought the real reason she was angry was 'cause he hadn't swooned over her yet, like most boys did.

"We're having a big day, too," he said. "Well, maybe I should say night."

The girls and I were surprised. We didn't think James and his friends did anything, just kind of hung around.

"What do you mean?" I asked. He had me curious.

James gave me a long look like he was deciding whether or not he'd even bother explaining. He must have made up his mind that we weren't total idiots 'cause he reached into his backpack and pulled out what looked like some flyers.

"Maybe this will help. You girls can read, right?"

Tori looked like she was going to jump down his throat, but I caught the wicked gleam in his eyes and knew we were being played.

"Eric and Noah here, me, of course, and a guy from St. Benedict's play in a band," he said. "We have a four week booking at Carino's Café. It's in …"

Tori interrupted, "Yeah, we know where it is." She looked at the flyer and then narrowed her eyes at him like she couldn't believe it. "You're a musician?"

He looked at his buddies. "We try to be."

"Our big chance might be next month when we audition for a gig at The Brown Door in Philly," Noah said, joining the conversation. He was a thin, sandy-haired boy who had such a baby face you'd think he was twelve. Noticing our blank faces, Noah explained that The Brown Door was a famous coffee house off South Street near Washington Square.

"On Sunday afternoons they open it up for new bands and a younger crowd," he said. "If we get the job it could be the break we need that can lead to other things."

I think we were all a little stunned. Ellen, Tori, and I had been sitting here for a week thinking life was all about us, and that we were stuck with these guys. Maybe they'd been thinking the same thing, like maybe they thought we were just a bunch of dumb athletes.

I had only been to Philadelphia a few times when I was little, doing the usual historic tour thing with the Liberty Bell and Betsy Ross house. I'd never even heard of the places that Noah was talking about and felt like a country hick, but since I didn't live in the country, make that a hayseed from the burbs.

I asked Noah what sort of music they played and he told me that it was kind of alternative.

"We're mostly a cover band, but we try to get in some of our own stuff, too," he said.

That sparked my interest. My brother had always been into indie music and riding to school with him last year kind of expanded my top-forty music taste.

The bell rang ending our conversation and when I left for class James was walking along side of me. I decided to ease up on my initial attitude and be friendly.

"So, James, who's the singer? What do you play?" I asked.

His eyebrows shot up, probably surprised at my sudden interest since I pretty much blew him off last week.

"I play guitar and keyboard when I'm with the band, but I like piano best," he said.

"Three instruments? Pretty impressive. That's three more than me," I said.

"So who sings?" I asked again.

"Mostly Noah and me. Eric is on drums. We kind of tell him to fake it since his range is well … you know … limited."

When we got to our English class I wished James good luck and he said the same to me. Taking my seat I had to wonder how it was that we knew so little of people that were all around us. Here these guys were doing something cool like being in a band and we were just ignoring them at lunch like they weren't even alive. Well, to be fair, they pretty much pretended we didn't exist either.

*It might be fun to hear their band play sometime. Even if they were lousy, it was still cool they were trying. I'll have to talk to the twins about it. Mitch, too.*

As I opened my book, I grinned to myself thinking that it might be good for Tori to have to do some chasing herself for a change, and I knew James had her interested.

*       *       *

When I got to the entrance to the locker room, Mitch was leaning against the wall, waiting for me.

"Just wanted to wish you luck, Reds."

"Thanks," I said, "but I'm only playing JV."

"It still matters. But if you do get into the varsity game give it all you've got. I'll call you tonight," he said, and started to leave.

He was so sweet to think that Mrs. Fortunato would put me in the varsity game that I momentarily forgot where I was and grabbed his arm to stop him. I leaned up and gave him a quick kiss. My impulse was probably not such a good idea, though, as Mandy and Kat were coming down the hall right behind me.

"Hey, no smooching on game day," Mandy called out. She walked up to Mitch and lightly knuckled his arm, "Drains the strength of our little hotshot, you know."

Mitch grinned and said good-bye. But I was mortified and quickly turned and made my way into the locker room. I thought I heard Kat call my name as I went through the door.

I was changing into my kilt when Mandy and Kat walked over to me.

"Cute guy, Jackie. Good for you," Mandy said.

"We were just teasing out there in the hall. No hard feelings, right?" Kat added.

I smiled. It was the first time Kat had even acknowledged my existence and I wondered if it was just because she was with Mandy who was always so nice to everyone. I said, "No problem," but decided there was no way I was ever going to get caught out again being all lovey-dovey in school.

*     *     *

Usually music for a pre-game warm up would have me bouncing, psyched for the game to start. Not this time. I felt the action swirling around me, but just couldn't find my usual fire. When Mrs. Fortunato read out the varsity lineup, my name, of course, was missing. Jules' was not. She was starting at left back. I was happy for her, but as she jogged out on the field for the opening whistle, and I was left on the sidelines, I felt confused and a little lost. I mean this was what I wanted, right? So what was my problem?

As the game got underway my feet started shifting back and forth. I couldn't stay still. It was then I realized that there was a part of me, deep inside, that wanted to be out there, too.

The score in the second half was 2-0, Northfield up, when Mrs. Fortunato called me over to put me in the game for Bri. Surprised, I thought Coach had given up on me by then. In the first half I'd been watching the girl that had been marking Bri. I noticed she'd been playing in front of Bri, intercepting everything being hit in Bri's direction. So as I ran out on the field I thought I knew how I could get to the ball first.

My plan worked and all of a sudden I was beating the girl to the ball. And, thanks to some great passes from Mandy and Jules, I was taking off down the field with the ball in my possession. I got a few good passes off to the other forwards and even took a shot myself. Surprisingly, Mrs. Fortunato left me in for the rest of the half.

In the after-game huddle, while we were giving the other team a cheer, I looked up and saw Bri staring back at me like I was poison. It made me shiver. And, for a moment, I wished Mrs. Fortunato would never put me in a varsity game again.

When I talked to Mitch that night I thanked him for how much he had helped me understand how to beat a defender to the ball.

He laughed, "Jackie, you're so easy to please. Most girls bug a guy for more attention or start pouting if he even speaks to another girl. Not you. If I keep coaching you, will you keep being my girl forever?"

"Of course, forever," I said, not even thinking about the significance of those words.

# - 18 -

On Saturday night my parents dropped me off at Mitch's house, and double-checked that his dad would bring me home. After we spent some time talking with his dad, Mitch and I walked down the street to Davey's house.

"I like your dress, Jackie," he said, as he took my hand.

Dresses were usually not my style, but the little green shift was pretty basic and I figured Mitch was worth me taking it up a notch sometimes.

Checking out Mitch in his fitted jeans and chest-hugging T-shirt, I thought he had to be one of the best looking guys in our class. And I wondered, and not for the first time, why he picked me.

As we got near Davey's house we could hear the music blaring. *Uh-oh,* I thought, *this party is going to rock.* It got me curious if Mitch was a dancer. Our school's semi-formal had been canceled last year because of a freak snowstorm so the opportunity had never come up.

Davey met us at the door and I could tell from the noise that the party was already in full swing.

"Come on out to the kitchen. I'll get you guys something to drink."

As we inched our way through the crowded hallway, I saw Jan, Davey's girlfriend, working her way toward us.

"Jackie, Mitch, what's happening?" she said.

She seemed genuinely glad to see us so I guessed I passed the 'not too much of a dork' test. When she gave me a hug I could smell the alcohol on her breath, though, and it made me feel a little uneasy. She gave Mitch a kiss on the cheek, which I didn't particularly like, but Jan didn't strike me as a flirt or boyfriend stealer, so I guessed it was just her way.

"What'll it be guys, soda, water?" She lowered her voice, "If you want a beer, there's a cooler out back, but you've got to watch out 'cause Mr. Barr is a heat-seeking missile when it comes to underage drinkers. Right, Davey?" She gave her boyfriend a nudge and he laughed.

I took a soda. Mitch hesitated and then he said he'd have a soda, "for now."

I gave him a look, *what did he mean, for now?* I'd never heard Mitch ever talk about drinking. Was this something new, something he started in Texas?

I didn't have time to think about it any further, though, as Mitch took me by the hand and led me through the back of the house and onto the deck. Most of the people we saw were strangers. I figured they must be friends of Davey's brother. Mr. and Mrs. Barr were somewhere as I had a glimpse of them, when I first came in, taking food out onto the deck.

"So what do you think … ?" Mitch started to say just as his two friends, Will and Kurt, came up behind him and gave him a little 'guy-pounding.'

"Hey, Jackie, I see he's finally letting you come out and see some real action," Kurt said, like what he did was much more fun.

I noticed both he and Will had a beer in their hands and Kurt seemed to be particularly happy right then. The music was pulsing in the background. I started to sway to the beat and gave Mitch a hopeful look 'cause I really wanted to dance. He didn't pick up on it, but Kurt didn't miss my signal.

"Come on, Jackie, the big dude has two left feet, but I think I can hang," he said.

Before Mitch could say a word, Kurt had me by the hand, pulling me out onto the deck's dance floor. I looked back at Mitch to see if this was okay with him, but he just laughed and said, "Have fun." As I joined Kurt in his gyrations, I knew my question had been answered. My boyfriend was not a dancer.

After a while the music started to slow, and as if by magic, Mitch appeared by my side and whispered in my ear, "My turn now. I think I can manage this one."

He wrapped his long arms around me. I leaned my face against his chest and smiled to myself – our first dance. I closed my eyes and his arms tightened around me. The moment more than made up for what we missed as freshmen.

We took a break from dancing and I sat up on the deck's railing to watch the other dancers while Mitch went to get me another soda. Kurt came over with a girl I didn't know, and asked me to hold his beer while he danced. Another kid bumped into him as he handed me the bottle, and beer splashed all over my dress.

"Oops," he laughed, and turned away like it was nothing major, leaving me stuck with his stupid beer. It couldn't have been more than thirty seconds later that Mr. Barr weaved through the crowd carrying some empty bottles and spotted me and the beer.

"Just what do you think you're doing, young lady?" he asked, grabbing the bottle out of my hand.

I started to tell him it wasn't mine, but he wasn't listening.

"I know your father. He's not going to be happy about this. You better leave." Then he said, "You do have a ride, don't you?"

I nodded and got down from the railing as my eyes filled up.

Tears rolling down my cheeks, I blindly weaved my way though the dancers, and finally made it to the kitchen where I saw Mitch talking with Davey and Jan. They all turned when they saw me approach.

"What's wrong, Jackie?" Mitch asked, and pulled me toward him. I stammered out the story. I was so afraid of what Mr. Barr would tell my parents. My dad would never believe I wasn't drinking when he saw my dress.

Jan looked down at the floor. I mean, what could she say? Davey mumbled something like he'd talk with his dad. I told Mitch we needed to get out of there.

We walked slowly back down the street. Mitch had his arm around me, trying to comfort me.

"Jackie, don't worry. I'll tell your dad what really happened."

I wiped at my wet face. *Maybe it wouldn't be so bad. Maybe Dad would believe Mitch and not Mr. Barr.* But I wasn't sure. I could get grounded forever if Dad thought I had been drinking. *Maybe he wouldn't even let me play hockey.*

On that thought I got all worked up again, and the tears started coming.

Mitch stopped and pulled me toward the shadow of a big evergreen tree. He held me for a long time, rubbing my back until I quieted down.

"You okay?" he asked, taking my chin in his hand and looking into my face. I nodded and looked up at him. He always made things seem so much better.

"I've got a better way to end tonight," he said softly. When his lips met mine I forgot everything. The party, Mr. Barr, it all just disappeared.

After a few moments, Mitch said against my cheek, "All better?"

I smiled into the dark – *maybe not all better, but definitely improved* and we started to walk again.

As we got near his house, I was surprised to see my parents' car in the drive. We hurried into the house, not knowing why they would be there, and if something was wrong. *Mr. Barr couldn't have reached them that fast!* My heart beat faster.

My mom and dad were sitting in the living room and when they saw us my dad stood up and said to Mitch, "Your father called us an hour ago. There was an emergency and he had to go back to the base."

"Is he okay?" Mitch asked.

I could see the instant worry on his face.

Dad tried to reassure Mitch that everything was fine, that it was just a military thing though he wasn't exactly sure what. That explanation seemed to relax Mitch so I guessed he was used to the mysterious 'need to know only' kind of absences.

My parents told Mitch his dad would call him in a while, and that they were going to take me home. He walked me out to the car and just before I slid into the back seat he gave me a quick kiss on the cheek.

"Thanks, Jackie. I had a great time."

I smiled back at him and when we were driving away I turned and looked out the back window and gave him a little wave. When I settled back in the seat, I thought Mitch was pretty grownup to be able to handle his father being called away all of a sudden like that. It's not like a father going to the hospital to do an emergency surgery. In the military there was always the chance of real danger. It came to me once again how different our lives really were.

As we pulled onto our street I realized my parents hadn't even noticed my dress. I breathed a sigh of relief. Maybe the worst was over.

# - 19 -

I didn't hear from Mitch the next day, so I assumed everything was okay at his house or he would have called. Every
time the phone did ring, though, I broke out in a sweat and
held my breath, thinking it might be Mr. Barr.

By Monday there had been no dreaded phone call. I figured I must be in the clear and that Davey had straightened it
out with his dad. As I headed to fourth period gym my mood
was definitely upbeat. I was really looking forward to seeing
Mitch.

As the class was walking out to the field for another
round of flag football, I hurried over to join him.

"What's up?" I said, realizing for the first time that he had
not come over to speak to me like he usually did.

He didn't look up, and when he spoke his eyes were still
focused on the ground. His voice sounded kind of unnatural
and strained when he said, "Long weekend. Listen, I'll call
you tonight." Then he walked quickly away, hurrying to catch
up with Kurt. Stunned, I slowed my pace and Lindsay and
Jules eventually caught up with me.

Lindsay looked at me, noticed my shocked face, and then
glanced at Mitch. "You guys have a fight?"

"No, I don't think so," I said, slowly shaking my head.

"What did he say?" Jules asked, knowing something had to be wrong.

"Nothing really. He said he would talk to me later. It seemed like he didn't have time for me." I felt numb. *He's never been like this with me. It's not like him and I don't know what to do. Do I try to talk with him, ignore him, or what?*

Mitch kept me at a distance for the rest of class and I was feeling completely miserable by the time I got to lunch. When I brought my tray to the table, Tori eyed my lone juice carton and apple, and said kiddingly, "Where's your famous appetite? You feeling sick?"

"I don't know, just not hungry."

She knew that this was not like me at all. She leaned forward and said more gently, "Seriously Jackie, you sound like you lost your best friend or something."

James must have overheard Tori 'cause I could feel him glance my way, but I just ignored him and crossed my arms on the table and put my head down.

"Maybe I'm coming down with something," I said. *Just leave me alone* is what I thought.

When I walked to English, James came up along side of me and said, "Maybe you should go to the nurse's office. You do look a little pale."

"No, I'm okay." *Snap out of it, stop being so sappy.* I forced myself to focus on something else. "So how did things go for your band over the weekend?"

"Okay, I think. At least they didn't throw anything at us," he said, and I could tell he was surprised I even remembered.

"Maybe my friends and I could see you guys sometime."

*Will that include Mitch? Is he going to break up with me? What is wrong?*

Sitting in class, my stomach getting more and more upset, I searched my memory for something that I might have missed on Saturday night, something that I did or said wrong. I couldn't come up with a thing.

For the first time ever I couldn't wait for hockey to be over, and when we were waiting for the late buses Jules said to me, "Maybe you're just reading too much into today. Everyone's entitled to a bad day, don't you think?"

I smiled at her positive spin. It lifted my spirits for one brief moment and as I got onto the bus I thought maybe I was making too much of things.

\*     \*     \*

After I finished my homework, I was sitting at my desk waiting for him to call. Worries were creeping back into my head and my stomach was beginning to churn up again. By nine o'clock I was even working up to the idea of cleaning out some drawers, just so I wouldn't go nuts, when my cell phone rang.

"Hey Jackie," Mitch said.

I held my breath waiting for what he was going to say next.

"Sorry I was such a jerk today," he said. "Look, we need to talk."

"Did I do something wrong?" I asked, worriedly.

"No, never. It's not you at all. It's me. It's my darn family. Can I come over for awhile tomorrow night?"

"Sure, Mitch. Will I see you in gym?"

"I'm not sure. I'll be there tomorrow night, though." And just like that he ended the conversation.

*     *     *

Getting through the games Tuesday afternoon was a chore. All I could think about was Mitch's visit. For the ten minutes I was in the varsity game I knew I didn't do anything on the field to impress Mrs. Fortunato. That was for sure. Bri was probably thrilled.

When I got home I let Mom know that Mitch was stopping by and she did the 'it's a school night' routine, but I assured her that it was really important and that he probably wouldn't be staying that long anyway.

His father dropped him off at seven-thirty and we went down the basement to talk. I led the way down the stairs. Looking back over my shoulder, I said tentatively, "Missed you in gym today," but his face didn't give me any clue as to what was going on.

When he got to the bottom step he reached for me and pulled me into his arms. "Don't say anything. Just let me hold you," he said.

It felt so nice to have his arms around me. I could feel his chin resting on the top of my head. I was sure there had been some simple misunderstanding and everything was going to be all right. Then suddenly his arms disappeared and he was leading me over to the couch, settling me in next to him.

He held my hand in both of his and seemed to be examining it, turning it over and back. It looked like he was trying to figure out what to say.

I watched his eyes studying my hand. After a moment he said, "Jackie, it's over."

My heart stopped, I know it did 'cause how could it beat when it was being squeezed into a tiny ball. This was the worst thing he could have possibly said.

Finally he looked at me and said, "I'm leaving ... tomorrow."

"What? What are you talking about?" I couldn't process what he was saying. Not we're through 'cause I don't like you anymore or I've found someone else. But, I'm leaving. My thoughts swirled. I suddenly felt cold.

"I can't stand this. It's just not fair," he said, with frustration, and he put his arm around my shoulder, and pulled me close.

He saw my eyes fill with tears and he reached up to blot them away. "Please don't cry. It only makes it worse."

"What's happened?" I finally got out.

"My dad has to go overseas on assignment. It's happened before. We just never thought with him being so close to retirement that he would be sent away again, but I guess things have gotten bad."

"Where?" I asked, feeling like this whole conversation was spinning out of control.

"He can never say. My mom is flying in tomorrow morning and withdrawing me from school. I'll be flying back with her tomorrow night and going to school in Texas, at least for the rest of the year."

"But you'll be back for next year, right?" I asked, hopefully.

"I can't count on that. I can't count on anything. I don't want you to think I'll be back. It wouldn't be fair. I'm sorry. Sorrier than I can say."

After a moment he looked at his watch. "My dad is waiting." He slowly brought his arms away from me and got up off the couch.

"You'll call, right? And we can still email each other," I said hopefully.

He shrugged his shoulders. He seemed so defeated. Then he said, "Tell your mom and dad good-bye for me." He leaned over and briefly kissed me, and without a backward glance, jogged back up the stairs.

I didn't follow him, but I heard the front door close. I looked around the room. This was where we ended our first date and where he gave me my first kiss. I felt my throat get tight and it was hard to breathe 'cause I realized this was the place of my last one, too.

Before I crawled into bed that night I paused by my bureau and looked down at my wrist. I gently removed my bracelet, wrapped it in some tissue paper, and slid it into the back of my top drawer. I looked down at the slight tan line on my arm where the bracelet had been and knew it would disappear more easily than my feelings for Mitch ever would.

# - 20 -

I would have given anything not to have to go to school the next day. I just wanted to stay under the covers and pretend the day before had never happened. It was such an effort to get dressed that I grabbed any old thing and didn't even bother blow-drying my crazy hair.

Mom was busy packing Lizzie's lunch and didn't notice me playing with my breakfast.

"Jackie, we missed seeing Mitch last night. He didn't stay long," she said. She turned away from the sink, expecting me to make a comment. Then she saw my face.

"What's wrong?"

"Mom." I could feel the tears forming and I wished I could just blink them away. "He's gone."

"What do you mean, gone?"

The words just came gushing out and I told her everything. Mom pulled up a chair next to me and wrapped her arms around me.

"I'm so, so sorry," she said.

"I keep thinking of Matt," I said, remembering again my brother's breakup with his girlfriend last fall. Matt had been a mess and it nearly destroyed his chances for a college soccer scholarship. When I tried to help him through it he reacted with such anger saying I didn't understand. I sure did now.

"I know you're going to miss Mitch, honey," Mom said. "But think about what he must be going through right now. His whole world has been turned upside down."

In my head I knew she was right, but logic didn't always help the heart and I felt like a big chunk of mine had gone missing. For once my mom got what I was going through since she was missing my brother so much. I never felt so close to her as I did that morning. She even volunteered to drive me to school.

When we arrived at Northfield and I started to get out of the car, Mom grabbed my hand and said, "Just focus on your hockey." That almost got the tears flowing again 'cause I knew what a big statement that was for my mom to make. And in that moment I wouldn't have traded her for any mother in the whole universe.

The day seemed to last forever and all I wanted was to go home and be alone in my room. My friends were sympathetic when I told them what happened. Jules was especially supportive, telling me I could call and vent anytime I wanted. Even Will and Kurt were unusually quiet in gym, so I knew they were missing him, too.

At my desk that night I realized I had to get to work on my English assignment. It was due the next day. I was feeling particularly sorry for myself sitting there and had a nose-dive moment when I imagined Mitch meeting some new girl, maybe having him take her, and not me, to some future dance. More than that, I missed him calling me that night, just checking in like he always did. That made me the saddest of all.

Slowly I started putting my emotions onto the computer screen. I didn't edit. I just let the feelings lie there on the screen. I paused a moment, not really looking at the words, hit print, and then slid into bed.

\* \* \*

After breakfast the next morning, I grabbed the sheet from the printer and was off. At school my classes seemed to drag on forever and I don't think I could remember a single thing any of my teachers said. At lunch James seemed to be debating whether to speak to me or not. I thought he was afraid to say anything to me, like if he did maybe I'd fall apart. He finally broke the silence.

"Hey, did you finish your assignment?"

"Yep, around ten. How about you?" I asked, just being polite. I gave him a small smile, surprised that the muscles in my face still could work in that direction.

He looked relieved, like maybe I wouldn't crumble after all. It suddenly came to me that boys really didn't function very well when they thought girls were going to cry.

"Oh yeah, I finished eons ago." He grinned sheepishly. "Actually, it's one of my old songs."

"Can we hear it?" Tori asked, joining in our conversation.

"No," James snapped, "you're not in the class. Anyway, it's supposed to be anonymous."

I gave him a quick look, hearing the change in the atmosphere. *What's going on? Have I missed something, stewing in my own stuff?*

I looked around the table. His band members were doing their best to look invisible, and Ellen looked as perplexed as I was.

The bell rang and James started to walk me to class. Despite my mood I was kind of curious to know what the deal was between him and Tori. However, I decided I was not ready for anymore drama right about then, so I kept silent as both of us walked down the hall together both lost in our own thoughts.

Mr. Barrows collected our assignments and we spent the rest of the class period mounting the papers on the walls around the room and then putting blank pages alongside them. Our job for the next two days was to take our time and go around the room writing comments on what we thought about the writing. Actually, we were not critiquing them as English assignments, but how the writing affected us. Even though I was pretty down I thought it was a cool idea.

I liked reading what everyone had to say. Some things were goofy and quirky. Some people kept things on the surface, not revealing too much, while others really touched me with what they wrote. One person described their dog dying and I thought of Mitch 'cause it was really all about loss. It wasn't just that the writer's dog was gone. It was about a relationship ending, too.

I left a note telling the writer how I really got it. I tried to figure out which paper belonged to James. I had it narrowed down to two possibilities, both written like poetry, and hoped maybe he'd eventually tell me. Next week we'd get our assignments back with all our classmates' comments, and I wondered if what I had written had made sense to anyone.

In practice I tried to pull myself together and put all my energy into the drills, but it didn't work. Even the hockey field, my second home, the place that let me disappear when things got too crummy, didn't help. I had nowhere to go.

*  *  *

As the days went on, I would look around in gym, half expecting to see him. Of course he wasn't there, but the memories were. Every time I saw Kurt or Will there seemed to be a missing piece, like he should have been by their side, laughing at Kurt's silly jokes or deep in conversation with Will sharing their love of sports.

I couldn't wait for the final bell of the day when I could be released from my thinking and let my excess energy loose on the field. Nighttimes were the worst. Sitting at my desk I would find myself staring at his picture instead of doing my reading, or looking at my silent phone willing him to call.

I tried to imagine what his new school might be like and if he was making friends. I figured he must have forgotten me pretty quickly not to hear anything and then I finally got an email – it was him.

He apologized for not calling. At first he thought it was best not to, and then he got into it with his mom and she took his cell phone away. He hated his new school. The only good thing was that the basketball coach had been in contact with Northfield's coach and had invited Mitch to try out for the team.

I answered his email, but afterwards I felt such a letdown. It reminded me too much that he was really gone and I'd never see him again. I went to bed that night in tears and woke the next morning emotionally exhausted.

*  *  *

I spent a week and a half in this no man's land. I was totally useless and barely got my homework in on time. The following Sunday I was still in bed, not really wanting to get up, when the front doorbell rang. My mom called up. "You have visitors."

A few moments later two human missiles launched themselves through the air, landing half on my bed and half on me.

"Ouch, you guys are killing me," I said, and couldn't help but smile as I tried to pull the covers up over me. Jules yanked the bedspread back and glared at me.

"And you are killing us," she said, sounding annoyed.

The comment stung. "What do you mean?"

"Our friend has disappeared and we want her back," Tori said softly.

I pushed myself upright against the headboard and crossed my arms over my chest. "That's not fair."

The twins flipped around, positioning themselves on either side of me like bookends, and I was trapped.

"We know you're sad about Mitch," Jules said. "It was lousy that he had to leave like that. But at least you're going to the same classes every day, seeing the same friends. He's not. He's going to have to start over and with a new basketball team, too. Did you ever think about that?"

I couldn't meet her eyes. I hadn't. It had been all about how I was feeling.

"Jules won't say this, but I will," Tori said. "The varsity needs you. They may be winning, but not by much. You've got to get out there and stop worrying about the stupid upperclassmen. You need to go kick some butt."

I started squirming under the sheets. *How does she know about the upperclassmen? Am I that obvious?* Their intervention, or whatever it was called, was not how I pictured my morning going.

"You have to quit this moping around," Jules said. "We'll be there for you. You just have to meet us halfway." She started to get off the bed. "Our mom's waiting for us, but we really needed to see you and say what was on our minds." She gave me a long look then moved toward the door.

Tori gave me a hug. "Mitch would never want you to be this way. Besides," she said, grinning as she went to join her sister, "there are still so many cute boys to meet."

I sat in bed for a long time after the twins left, letting what they said play through my mind. One thing I knew they were right about. Mitch would be disappointed if I didn't give hockey my best.

By now I was only playing JV, which made total sense 'cause I sure hadn't shown Mrs. Fortunato anything. Then on Tuesday, Northfield had a game with our crosstown rival, St. Benedict's. The varsity played terribly, even arguing among themselves out on the field. They barely escaped with a tie. But, what made it even worse was what happened afterwards, in the locker room.

After getting changed I walked down a couple of rows to get some water and saw Mandy at the end of an aisle sitting by herself with her face in her hands. I was pretty sure she was crying.

As I got back to my locker to pick up my things I overheard Bri and some of her friends laughing and joking around about the game, like the way they played wasn't such a big deal. Bri said, "I don't know what Mandy is so upset about. It's not like we lost."

Riding home on the bus I kept playing the picture of Mandy over and over, and then thought about some of the other girls' reactions and started to simmer. My emotions kept building and by three o'clock the next day I was boiling. Over the next three practices I played like a maniac. All I wanted was to get to goal and hear the sound of the ball pounding into the backboards.

I felt like a human matchstick – a nerve was struck and I was on fire. I caught Jules' eye at one point and she had the biggest grin on her face. She didn't say anything to me, though. Probably thought it'd be bad karma.

*     *     *

On Saturday, the team had an out-of-conference game with a big powerhouse school from North Jersey. It meant a two hour bus trip which I wasn't looking forward to, but at least we could catch up on our sleep. Unfortunately the trip gave our coach an opportunity for her famous 'in-depth' talks with the players. I was the fourth one called up to the hot seat in the front of the bus. It surprised me since I didn't really think I was on her radar screen anymore.

I settled in next to her and she asked, "So, Jackie, how are things going for you?"

For a moment I wasn't sure what she was talking about. *She couldn't mean about me and Mitch, could she?*

She studied me, waiting for a reply.

"Uh, okay I guess," I said, finally realizing she must be talking about hockey. I thought that was a good enough answer, but I could tell she was waiting for me to say more.

How was it, I wondered, that silence could mean a whole lot of words were being said without a sound coming out of a person's mouth?

A few weeks ago I would have been all fidgety sitting there, but I knew Coach a little better now or maybe my head was just in a different place. I let out a breath and started talking.

"At first I didn't understand why I wasn't getting the ball, but some people helped me out and now I get how much you have to do to get open. I'm still working on the timing thing though," I said.

She smiled at me. "You seemed a little up and down for a couple of weeks, but you've had really good practices the last couple of days. I know there's a big difference between freshman ball and varsity, especially for a forward, but I think you're catching on."

I brightened a little.

Mrs. Fortunato went on, "So, do you think you're ready to start today?"

I looked away for a moment. I knew she meant varsity. *Mitch would be so happy for me right now.* I took a big swallow, then turned back to face her.

"Yes, I think I am."

"Good," she said, and then changed the subject. "How's it going with helping Ellen now that she's back? She certainly seems to be making up for lost time."

I grinned. It was so much easier than I thought. "Yeah, she's doing great," I said. "She really pays attention when you tell her stuff."

To Mrs. Fortunato it seemed like my reply was a no-brainer, like, of course, players would listen to me. Suddenly she shifted gears. Maybe she had gotten all she needed from me and was ready to move on 'cause then she asked me to have Tori come to the front of the bus.

I walked back to my seat and passed by Bri and her friend, Allison. Bri looked up and gave me a dirty look, and I wondered what she would say when she found out I was starting instead of her. As I took my seat I thought that talking with Coach and starting in the game was just the medicine I needed to get my life back on track. And as the bus exited the Turnpike and went through the toll booth, I knew if I stopped to take a peek inside my heart Mitch would still be there, and I could still feel my anger lurking in the shadows – toward his family for splitting up, the fighting overseas that took his father away, and just fate I guessed. But now I needed to get going and make hockey my focus, for a few hours anyway. The rest of my life – that would take some work.

# - 21 -

On Sunday, I decided to go for a long bike ride. I rode at an easy pace, slowly letting my mind unwind, and wound up pedaling to the top of Bowman's Hill, a local lookout. I leaned my bike against an old oak tree and plopped down to admire the view of the town below.

Off in the distance was my elementary school. I remembered my first days going there, tagging after my brother. That got me thinking about him leaving for college, my mom missing him so much, and how she needed to keep busy so she wouldn't be too upset. Maybe her fixing up his old room for me had helped her see no matter how sad things were, life had to go on. I wondered if I could do something like that, something that would heal the soreness in my heart.

Sitting at the lunch table on Monday I asked Noah if they were still playing at the café.

"Yep, we have one more week left. You should come."

"What do you think?" I asked Tori. I assumed she would reject the idea since she and James seemed to be bumping heads. So, I played to her sympathy.

"It might be good for me doing something different so I won't think about Mitch so much." I tried to mimic Lizzie's little-girl pleading, figuring it would help give Tori a case of the 'guilts' so she'd have to say yes.

"You should come too, Ellen," I added.

"That's a great idea," Ellen said. "Maybe I'll ask Danny."

James finally arrived at the table and as he sat down he caught the end of our conversation. "Who's Danny?" he asked.

"My boyfriend. He goes to St. Benedict's," Ellen said.

"Oh yeah? What year?" Eric asked.

"Junior," she said.

"Same as us, except of course for baby James," Noah said, with a teasing grin. James turned and threw a roll at Noah. It was a miss.

Noah laughed at James, "Relax, you know you're a whole lifetime ahead of us anyway."

"What does that mean?" I asked.

"Nothing," James said, obviously annoyed with Noah's comment. "He doesn't know what he's talking about."

I turned back to Tori, "So, you'll go?"

She looked nonchalant, but I knew her mind was working. "Maybe," she said, reluctantly. I thought her hesitation was more for James' benefit, not letting on she might be interested. Then again, I could have been imagining that.

*     *     *

In English we got our papers back. Clipped to the back were the comment pages. I got an A. *YES!* The notes left by the other students were pretty positive. One was especially intriguing. It said, "I'd like to talk with you about this," and it was just signed with the letter J. I looked up at James to see if he was watching my reaction, but he was going through his own papers.

After class I had a few minutes before biology, so I snagged James as he was walking to the door. "Are you J?"

As we passed through the door he said, "Yeah, it was good stuff, Jackie. I'd probably need to make a few changes, but I'd like to use what you wrote as a song." He saw my confusion. "Seriously, I would give you credit, like co-publish it."

"How, how'd you know it was me?" I stuttered.

"I'm not totally clueless. Your boy leaving Northfield really had to stink."

I was embarrassed he knew my deepest feelings about Mitch and the emptiness I felt, so I tried to play it off. "Well, you can just have it," I said.

He shook his head and said, "No, that's not right. It has to be both of us together or not at all."

"Okay, but my part is already done, right?"

"Sure, sure," he said, laughing, "but if I can get it to work I'll give you final approval, okay?"

I nodded my head too stunned to speak. On one hand I was flattered he liked it, but on the other – the pain part – I just wanted to put it behind me. When we came to the beginning of C wing, I waved good-bye, and hurried down the hall to science class.

The rest of the day went quickly and after practice I cornered Tori in the locker room and made her promise that she'd go hear the band play on Friday night. I decided that when I got home I would mark my calendar with a big circle. The night was to be a new beginning. I was determined not to look back.

*     *     *

By Friday our group had grown and included the twins, Ellen and Danny, Lindsay, and a friend of Danny's from St. Benedict's who knew the drummer in the band. We told the boys at lunch that we were coming to see them play and James seemed surprised.

"Do we have to buy dinners or something?" I asked.

"No, no, nothing like that," Noah said. "There is a five dollar cover charge, though, and if you buy something to drink that's good enough. They do have a real good dessert bar."

The thought of desserts made me smile. I figured that something sweet had to be a good omen, like maybe I could get through all this.

*     *     *

The twins had talked their brother Chris into driving us that night, and as we got near the place, he told us that he'd be back around ten.

"Why don't you come with us?" I asked.

I caught Jules giving him a sideways look and he shook his head.

"No, that's okay, maybe another time," he said.

"Yeah, what was I thinking, you probably have all your dates lined up for the evening, a new one every hour," I said, laughing. "We could seriously mess up your schedule."

He looked at me through the rearview mirror. "Your opinion of me is way off, Jackie McKendry," he said.

"Right," I said, looking back at him in the mirror with a grin on my face. I mean you just had to look at him and know he'd have no shortage of girls.

Once we paid the cover charge at the door we took our time looking around the place. I'd only been there a few times for lunch with my mom, so I didn't really know what it was like at night. There were about fifteen to twenty tables with checkered tablecloths and lit candles on each table. The lighting was turned down. Toward the back there was a small raised stage where I could see the boys setting up. Most of the tables near the stage were already filled with people having dinner.

We grabbed two tables away from the stage and asked the waitress if we could put them together. Ellen came in with Danny and the other boy from St. Benedict's a few minutes later. Everybody was introduced and I realized I was right to push for this. It was exactly what I needed. I wondered briefly what Mitch was doing on his Friday night in Texas, but forced my mind back to this café, determined to enjoy the company around me.

The waitress took our orders. My mouth was already watering for the chocolate layer cake I had checked out in the glass case near the entrance. I glanced to the stage and noticed the boys had their instruments tuned and the place was starting to fill up.

The band opened with some cover songs. James and Noah did a lot of the harmony. Noah's voice was sweet and sure. It was a good contrast to James' more husky sound. Then James did a solo, a song I'd never heard before. As he sang, all the clatter of the knives and forks stopped and there was silence throughout the little room.

He sure didn't seem like the boy we sat with at lunch every day. He really had a gift of taking the audience on a journey with him. I couldn't be sure if it was his voice or the lyrics that made me feel this way, but I knew that he was really good and was totally sure of himself on the stage. The next two songs involved the whole band, and James faded away, just another member of the group.

The band took a break and Noah wandered over to our tables. "Hey guys, thanks for coming." Ellen and I gushed how good we thought the band was, and he smiled, pleased. Actually everyone seemed to like what they'd heard. "I'll tell the guys," he said.

"Isn't James coming over?" I asked.

"Maybe later. He likes to keep to himself while he's performing." He looked over his shoulder, "I better get back. See you guys."

"What do you think, Tori?" I asked. Ellen looked at me and smiled at my question. I knew she had felt the vibes that had been going on at our lunch table.

"They're not bad, I'll give them that," Tori said, like it hardly mattered to her.

Jules looked at her like she was nuts. "They're way more than that, and that James is really terrific. He's in your lunch, right?" she asked, looking at me.

I nodded. *Uh-oh, Jules is showing some interest. Whoa! What'll happen if both she and Tori like the same guy? Maybe my innocent little night out could backfire and become a sisterly slugfest.* Of course I didn't know if James was even interested in Tori for sure. I just knew she got under his skin. Ellen and I exchanged another glance and I thought we were both thinking the same thing.

At the end of the band's second set, the boys came over to our table and everyone was introduced. James was a little more withdrawn than usual, but I did see him do a double take when he met Jules. I guess he didn't know Tori was a twin. James and Jules talked for a few minutes. Just before the boys went back to the stage to pack up, they thanked us for coming, and I thought they really meant it.

*     *     *

The next week was hectic with tons of school work. Normally I got a little whiny with the homework thing, but I knew I needed to keep busy so I wouldn't fall apart dwelling on the piece of my life that was missing.

I started in the next two games and we won, barely. Some of the players seemed to accept me starting in place of Bri, but others didn't. I was pretty sure those players were still avoiding passing me the ball. My being out on the field instead of Bri was just a small part of it, though. We just weren't jelling, and I had the feeling that making the team as strong as possible wasn't on everyone's priority list.

Coach was starting to play Tori a little bit and had moved her to the forward line. Even Sam Jones was seeing some time. The upperclassmen were beginning to grumble. I made up my mind to turn a deaf ear to the whole thing. A few weeks ago their attitude would have upset me, but not now. Losing Mitch and then seeing how much Mandy and some of the others wanted the team to be successful changed my whole attitude. I wasn't going to put up with the girl-drama anymore.

*     *     *

My progress in taking care of my aching heart stumbled a bit on Thursday night. I found another email from Mitch on my computer. He wrote that he really missed me and wondered why he hadn't heard from me in the last few days. That started my tears flowing again.

It was getting so painful trying to maintain some casual kind of connection. I felt like everything had been taken out of my control a few weeks ago and I just couldn't seem to be halfway about my feelings. Yet, I couldn't bring myself to say all that, so I just replied that things were okay and hit the send button.

# - 22 -

The following week found us smack in the heart of our conference schedule and our lineup was still not settled. A bunch of us found out that Mrs. Fortunato had a major meeting with the seniors after Saturday's practice.

We didn't know exactly what was said, but we could guess. We were sure some of the seniors felt they should automatically be in the spotlight and the season should be all about them. I cringed to think what Mrs. Fortunato would do if she realized this was their attitude 'cause she had a 'team first' philosophy for sure.

Before Tuesday's game Mrs. Fortunato brought the whole team together. "I've thought about this long and hard," she said. "I know some of you may be upset, however I cannot accept the effort I am getting from this team. This is today's starting lineup."

She read it out. Tori, Sam, and I were the new front line. As I jogged out on the field, I could feel the daggers flying from the benched players, but they weren't aimed just at me. Coach had made huge changes. There were six sophomores now starting for Northfield.

Coach was taking a huge chance with so many inexperienced players. I guessed she must have believed in us, but more importantly I thought she was making a case for what she stood for – that a team needed everyone trying their best and nothing less would do. I kind of liked that attitude in a coach and my respect for her grew even more.

The first half was a little bumpy. We all were feeling nervous and maybe trying a bit too hard. I thought at halftime she'd replace a lot of us with the older girls, figuring she'd taught them a lesson. But she didn't.

Ten minutes into the second half I got a sweet pass from Sam, and took off down the field. As I got near the circle I saw Sam and Tori with just one defender between them. I yelled to Sam, "Go through, go through," and as she ran on a diagonal across the circle, the lone defender slid over to mark her. That left Tori open. I put the ball right behind Sam to the open space, and Tori, surprised at my pass, just automatically reached out with her stick to stop the ball from going out of bounds. The ball popped off her stick and into the cage.

I couldn't remember if Tori had ever scored a goal before. She blinked and didn't move when the ref's whistle signaled goal. Sam and I ran over and jumped all over her.

"Hey wake up. You scored," I yelled.

All of sudden Tori came out of her coma and grinned, "Yeah, I really did." That was our only score, but it was a turning point for Tori who had always been in Jules' shadow on the athletic field.

Our season continued on and Coach kept the same new lineup. We weren't successful in every game, but didn't do badly either. All of us sophomores were slowly getting stronger and a good part of that was due to Mandy and Kate's patience while we were sorting through our growing pains.

Not once did they jump on us for our inconsistent play and eventually things started to click.

*   *   *

By the end of our season our conference record was 10-1-2 putting us in first place in the Mid-American Conference, North Division. The top team in the Mid-American, South Division was to be our opponent for the conference championship. As we went into that game I was our team's leading scorer. Sam was close behind, but there was no jealousy about who was putting the ball in the cage. All that mattered was that the ball got there.

Playing that game was probably our best effort of the season, one of those days where everyone brought their "A" game, and I thought us sophomores finally had earned our coaches' faith in us. We won 3-0 and with it, the conference championship. The trophy we received would be placed in our school's showcase alongside all the others. I was excited to know that I was part of the team putting it there.

Coach talked to us after the game, telling us how proud she was, and then announced that we had qualified for the state tournament. Winning 'states' was the desire of every good hockey program in New Jersey. A state committee ranked all the teams based on their wins and losses and then matched the strongest teams with the weakest in the opening rounds with the assumption that the strongest teams would prevail.

Since our record was pretty decent we were ranked high and our first opponent definitely lacked our speed and stick skills. We played them at home and beat them 5-0. A lot of our players got into the game as the clock ran down and I was especially glad for all the seniors, even the ones that hadn't been that nice.

The tough thing about state tournament was there were no second chances. If we lost a game we were done. For us sophomores there would always be other seasons, but for the seniors each game could be their last time in Northfield blue and white.

We talked about the seniors at lunch on Wednesday. We decided that we should decorate their lockers for Friday's second-round game.

"We'll ask Mrs. Fortunato to show us where their lockers are and give us a list of all the team members," Tori said.

The boys were listening to us and Noah said, "That's so cool what you're doing. We're sorry we missed your first game. Maybe we can get to this one. It's only fair since you came to hear us." Then he nudged James, "Hey, tell them our good news."

We all turned expectantly to James who was scowling at Noah. "It's no big deal."

"What do you mean no big deal?" Noah exclaimed. "We got the gig in Philly. We auditioned last night."

"Wow, that's great. You're all so good," said Ellen.

"When will it be?" I asked James.

"The end of January, a Saturday night and a Sunday afternoon," Noah said when James hadn't answered my question.

Later James and I were walking to class like always when I asked him, "It doesn't seem like you want us to see you play?"

He didn't look at me, but continued gazing down the hall. Finally he said, "It's hard to explain." He paused and rubbed the back of his neck searching for what he wanted to say next. Then he looked at me and said, "It's just that I feel better playing to strangers. I guess you could say, freer ... like I can be anyone when I don't know who's out there."

"Well, we won't go if you don't want us to."

"Let me think about it, okay?" He brightened up then, "Say, I'm working on that song of ours. I'm hoping to put it in the program for January."

"Unreal," I said, surprised. I thought he had given up on it since he hadn't mentioned it for ages.

"Why can't every girl be as easy to talk to as you?" he asked suddenly.

Surprised, I smiled, but couldn't give him an answer. I thought maybe stuff between a guy and girl was like an equation. Like no sparks equaled simple and straightforward. I wondered for a minute if it was one of the things I might have missed in basic algebra.

As we reached our classroom door and I shifted my knapsack to my other shoulder, James muttered, "I wish one of your friends was as easy to talk to."

I perked up at this offhanded remark. *Was he thinking of Tori?* I waited for him to say more. Instead, he shoved his hands deep into his pockets and quickly made his way across the room taking his usual seat by the window.

*       *       *

Tori bumped into Kate in the hallway and told her our plans for the seniors. By the time practice was over Kate had assigned all of the juniors and sophomores a senior. Jess, Lindsay, Anna, and I had Kat. I couldn't wait to go to the drugstore and pick out stuff.

As soon as we arrived at school on Friday we rushed to Kat's locker and quickly taped up the signs that we'd made with her uniform number and motivational sayings. We added a picture of her favorite movie actor to the locker with a pretend personal autograph saying he wished her the best of luck and wanted a date if she won.

"She'll love it," Anna said, and we all smiled in agreement.

By the afternoon the weather had turned bitter and windy. I was thankful for the cold gear under our uniform shirts. Some of the girls even wore running tights. I wasn't into wearing anything on my legs, but I had brought gloves since I knew it could really sting when you hit the ball in cold weather.

Before the game the seniors thanked us for decorating their lockers. Kat laughingly said, "We have to win because I've got a really hot date planned." Most of the team didn't know what she was talking about and some of us kept our heads lowered. We couldn't help but smile.

Because it was the second round of the tournament we knew this game would be a tighter contest. On paper we were expected to take it, but reputation didn't mean much once you were out on the field. Even though the first half was going our way, we just couldn't seem to put the ball in the cage. I was pretty confident that as the game wore on we **would** get the job done.

In the second half the other team made a defensive change. I couldn't figure it out at first, but it seemed like they had one defender in front of me and another player defending the space behind me. I really felt stifled every time I tried to make a move to the ball. After a while I gave up and decided that if two players were going to guard me it left more space for someone else on my team so I stayed away from the ball as best I could.

As the minutes ticked on, the game started to bog down and get physical with a lot of pushing and shoving. Mandy suddenly took off after a loose ball, trying to turn the game our way, and in a heartbeat our season was over. As she reached for the ball, a player from the other team inadvertently took her out from behind and they both went down. Mandy got the worst of it, and we heard her scream. It was chilling. I turned to look at her clutching her knee. I knew it wasn't good.

The refs took a time-out and the trainers and coaches rushed out to help her. There was no denying it – she was done. It took ten minutes before they could even get her to the sidelines.

It took the heart out of us, seeing her like that, and no one on the team could lead us like Mandy. With time running down on the clock the other team started to barrage Beth with shots and one finally found the back of the cage. It was the game-winning goal.

Afterwards we had to give them a cheer and then line up to shake their hands. It was so hard to look into their smiling faces while tears were rolling down our own. The seniors were crushed. I felt the weight of all the 'could-haves' and 'should-haves.' Regret was everywhere. Walking over to the bench to collect my things, I saw Coach hugging Mandy who had refused to be taken to the hospital until the game was over. She sure had given our team everything she could.

I never wanted to feel that way again – so unfinished. Right then I decided two things. One, we had failed the seniors. Two, before we graduated our class was going to win a state championship.

# - 23 -

A week after that final state game we turned in our uniforms. *How had it gone so fast?* It seemed unreal. I couldn't wrap my head around the fact the season was over. It was such an empty feeling.

Thanksgiving was a few weeks later, and my family was finally all together. Grandma McKendry was visiting from the shore and Matt was home from college. It was good to have him back, and I figured he must have missed us just as much as we missed him. It turned out what he missed most was our washer and dryer. Mom had to open the laundry room window to air out the place. I wondered how it was that my brother had turned into such a total slob in just three months.

Once he had the laundry under control Matt spent the whole break on the phone texting his new college friends or going out with his former soccer buddies from Northfield. We did talk briefly on Thanksgiving morning, and I told him all about Mitch. While he felt bad that Mitch had to leave school and go back to Texas, he thought it would be good for me to meet some other boys.

"You guys were way too serious," he said, and maybe he was right, but I had expected a little more sympathy after all the struggles he had when his girlfriend broke up with him last year. I could feel my brother pulling away as if what was going on at home wasn't all that important anymore.

Right before I got into bed that night I checked my email. There was another message from Mitch. He had wished me a Happy Thanksgiving and wrote a little bit about basketball. I was yanked right back to the night he left and felt the same heartache all over again. I leaned forward at my desk and put my hand up to the monitor. For a moment I felt the connection all the way to Texas. Then I slowly pulled my hand away to brush away the tears running down my face. "I'm sorry," I said, looking at the screen, "I can't do this anymore, forgive me." I would not read any more of his messages. I would simply hit 'delete.'

*     *     *

In the beginning of December we had our final field hockey event. It was Northfield's Fall Sports Awards Night. It was held in our school's auditorium. When it was Mrs. Fortunato's turn to talk about the varsity we stopped fidgeting in our seats and quieted down.

She mentioned a little something about each senior and they came up onto the stage where they each received a bouquet of flowers. If it was their first time on varsity they each received their varsity letter. Even though some of them didn't play much in the varsity games it was our school's policy to award them a letter for hanging in there for four years. Mandy was the only player to receive Northfield's three-year varsity award – a wristwatch. I looked down at my bare arm and figured I could be wearing that watch someday, too.

Next, Mrs. Fortunato called up the rest of us who were on varsity and gave us our letters. After we all took our seats again, Coach talked about the season and then it was time to recognize special honorees. Mandy, of course, was our Most Valuable Player. Then Coach announced the Northfield players who made our conference's all-star teams. Our Mid-American Conference chose both a first and a second team to represent the best of the conference's fourteen schools.

I was busy running my hand over my varsity letter, trying to imagine where I would put it in my room, when Coach read out the players that made the second team. I barely heard her when she said – "Kate Carson, Jules Hanson, and Jackie McKendry."

Lindsay poked me when she saw me not moving. "Get going," she said, and started to push me out of my seat.

I couldn't believe my name was called. I stumbled over two of my teammates to get out to the aisle, then hurried down toward the stage feeling that there must be some mistake and that all of a sudden Coach was going to say something like, "Oops, my bad, go sit down Jackie."

Instead, I kept walking toward her. She smiled and shook my hand, "Well done, Jackie, and certainly deserved."

Everyone clapped for us. Jules, standing next to me, nudged me, "See I told you we could do it." I knew she meant making varsity. Neither of us ever figured we'd be all-stars.

Mandy and our goalkeeper, Beth, were selected to the first team. This time Mandy remained on the stage after Coach called her up. She had just returned to school the week before following her knee surgery. And as she stood at the podium she gamely tried to balance her awards with her crutches. She took the microphone and spoke about the season and our coaches. It was so inspirational. Listening to her, I was so proud to have known her and a little piece of my brain recognized that she must have sat in these seats as a lowly sophomore, too, and in the blink of an eye her high school career had come to a close.

*     *     *

A few days later, after lunch, I was walking with James to English class and he said, "I'm done."

"Huh?"

His raised eyebrow shot me a special meaning. "You mean the song?" I asked. I had almost forgotten about it.

"Yep," he said, his eyes bright with excitement. He suggested we meet in the music room the next day and he'd bring his guitar.

The next afternoon hearing my words being sung, even though they were slightly changed around, was pretty incredible.

"James, that was wonderful," I said, as I watched him pack away his guitar.

"It was all your idea," he said, as he locked the case.

"I have to say my thoughts were pretty much on overload the night I wrote that," I said hesitantly.

He nodded like he understood. "How're you doing?" he asked.

"Okay, I don't let myself think about it. It doesn't do me any good."

"I get it," he said. And I wondered if anything like that had happened to him.

"Can I ask you something?" he said, as he turned off the lights and started to walk me down the hall.

"Sure."

"Do you think it's alright to call somebody if somebody they're close to might not like it?"

I was puzzled for a minute. Then it dawned on me – Tori and Jules. It took me a moment to answer him. I remembered the conversation I had with my mom last year about taking risks and how it finally made me decide to take a chance with Mitch. I would have missed so much joy.

"Go for it," I told him enthusiastically. "Maybe both people need to hear where you stand."

He seemed to be twirling my words around in his head for a minute. Then picking up his guitar case he said, "Do you have the Hansons' phone number?"

*     *     *

The next day I arrived at lunch anticipating a change in the air at our table. I looked expectantly at Tori and James – nothing. I wondered what was going on.

After lunch I got James alone in the hall. I was salivating with curiosity. "So, did you call?"

"Dying to know, huh," he said, with a smug grin on his face, and kept on walking.

"James," I called after him with exasperation, and hurried to catch up. He laughed and told me he did call the Hansons – and asked to speak to Jules.

*Wow*, I thought.

"She's going to meet me at the ice rink Friday night," he said.

"Good for you," I said. As we walked into English I had my fingers crossed that this wouldn't put a wedge between my two best friends, but I also was happy for Jules. Tori had run through enough guys already. For once it should be Jules' turn.

Tori called me that night and asked if I wanted to go to a basketball game with her at St. Benedict's on Friday. "It'll just be me and my mom. Jules bailed out on me 'cause she's meeting up with James," she said.

That's all she said about it and I decided, however they hashed it out, it was really none of my business and the less said the better. I agreed to go with her and her mom. It would be the first game I would see Chris play this year and I was sure it'd be fun.

*   *   *

St. Benedict's gym was filled to the rafters. The school's black and gold colors were everywhere.

"Big game, huh?" I said to Tori.

"Yeah, Chris is fired up. He's glad you could come," Tori said as she kept her eyes focused on the two teams warming up on the court.

I looked at her funny. Like, what would he care? But I figured he probably just enjoyed having a big crowd at the game. I noticed that Mrs. Hanson was very quiet as she glanced back and forth between her husband and Chris. It must be hard when things didn't go well. I mean, how can you want your husband yelling at your kid just because the game was a loss or your kid plays crummy? Or maybe you're mad at your own kid because he made your husband lose the game. Boy, I was glad my parents didn't coach anything.

There were no worries that night. Chris scored twenty-nine points and his team beat the visitors by fourteen, a double win for Mrs. Hanson.

We waited around after the game to meet up with Chris and his dad. When they came out of the locker room there was someone with them. The third person turned out to be a good friend of Chris's named Dean Rickert who also played for St. Benedict's. After we congratulated the guys on the game, Chris looked over to me, grinned, and keeping his eyes locked on mine said, "We're starving, but I'm pretty sure there is one other person here that needs to be fed, too."

I stuck out my tongue at him. My enormous appetite might be well known, but he really didn't have to bring it up in front of his friend. Chris chuckled at my response, picked up his gym bag, turned and headed to the exit.

Going out like this after a basketball game was a blast. Everyone was upbeat 'cause of the win. Most importantly, it was another new memory to be made without Mitch.

Once we were seated at the restaurant, Dean started up on me, asking me a ton of questions about myself, while Chris, who sat across from me, arms folded, looked amused. Mr. Hanson seemed relaxed and happy, too. I guessed for him this was a good early-season win to get under his belt. But I'd seen him in darker moods, and I'd rather have ten Mrs. Fortunatos on a bad day than one Mr. Hanson.

When we were leaving the restaurant, the boys were to ride with Mr. Hanson, and us girls with Mrs. Hanson. Before they got into the car, Chris turned to me and said, "Thanks for coming. Hope you enjoyed the game."

"You were terrific out there," I said, deciding I had already forgiven his earlier teasing.

He seemed pleased and his friend, Dean, slapped him on the back, whispered something to him, then turned to me and said, "Nice to meet you. See you around sometime."

On the way home we stopped off at the skating rink and picked up Jules. She slid into the back seat with me. I wanted to interrogate her and find out how much she liked James, but I still didn't know for sure what Tori's feelings were. I felt like the whole topic was off limits and it was frustrating. Fortunately, Mrs. Hanson asked Jules if she had fun. She glanced at her sister who was looking straight ahead, turned, and winked at me, "Yeah, it wasn't too bad."

*   *   *

On Monday I was still torn on how to treat the so-called Tori, Jules, James triangle. I wanted to be supportive of Jules, but I didn't want to offend Tori by taking sides. At lunch, James seemed a little more at ease with Tori and we were all relieved that she hadn't bitten his head off yet.

Eventually Tori put her fork down, and said, "Okay, I have an announcement to make." James slowly turned his head towards Tori and the rest of us froze in place, wondering what she'd say next. Tori continued, "It seems that James here has decided to court my sister. And, James, since you're a fairly competent musician, and seem to be relatively intelligent, I've decided you may be worthy of her. So I just wanted to let you know, you have my blessing."

We all looked to James unsure of how he would take Tori's theatrics. He grinned and said, "Gee thanks, Tori. It goes without saying that we plan to name our first born after you."

Noah, who must have been holding in a mouthful of fish sticks the whole time, was laughing so hard he started to choke. Eric had to slam him on the back a couple of times and food spurted all over the table. Then everyone was laughing and grabbing napkins trying to clean up the mess. Me, I knew the real mess here had already been cleaned up.

\*　　\*　　\*

The Christmas holiday came and went, but one night during vacation I reached into the back of my bureau drawer and unwrapped the tissue holding my copper bracelet. It was as bright and shiny as the day I first put it on. Looking down at my empty wrist I found that I couldn't see the tan line anymore that had showed where I had worn it. It dawned on me that there was some sort of symbolism going on. Like maybe the bracelet was really part of my past now, and should no longer have any impact on me. Then I slowly slipped the bracelet back into its resting place, wishing that my heart could accept what my brain had already logically concluded.

# - 24 -

In the middle of January the boys at our table were talking about their upcoming debut at The Brown Door in Philly.

"You guys should come," Noah said.

I glanced at James to see what he thought about the idea since the first time we had talked about it he wasn't so sure. He gave me a crooked grin and a subtle thumbs-up so I turned back to Noah.

"I don't even know how to get to Philly," I said.

I think you can take the high-speed line," he said, "but it might be better to drive if you come at night."

I was kind of doubtful that my parents would let me take the train. It sounded like fun, though. "We'll see," I said.

Tori called me that night, "Do you still want to go see the band?"

"Yeah, but I don't think I'll be allowed."

"Suppose I can get my brother to drive us. Then maybe your parents would let you go. You know he wouldn't let anything happen to us."

I thought that might work. I was sure my parents trusted Chris, so maybe if he drove it would be okay.

"I'll check and let you know. Do you think he'll do it? I mean it's a Saturday night, he might be busy."

"He could probably be bribed, if we pay him enough. Don't worry about it. He likes music, too, you know."

"Yeah, right. I forgot that."

*    *    *

It turned out to be okay with my mom and dad, and on the night of our trip to Philly I was still figuring out what a person should wear to a coffee house when the doorbell rang. It was Jules. "Come on up," I yelled, "I'm not ready." In a moment I was eyeing her jeans and lightweight fleece.

"I know it's cold out, but I'm sure the coffee house is warm and Chris has the heater going in the car," Jules said, as we looked through my closet. We decided that I'd wear jeans, too, and then we picked out a new white lacy stretch top that I had gotten for Christmas. Putting it on, I wondered if it was a little too formfitting and I thought maybe I should wear something over top of it. Jules gave me a look saying that it would defeat the purpose, whatever that meant. She said that as long as I had my parka I'd be warm enough.

We raced downstairs and I grabbed my coat and gloves. We hurried out to the car and both of us slid into the back seat. Chris turned to us and said good-naturedly, "It took you long enough." As he put the car in gear and headed down the street he chuckled, "Jackie, it's not a dance or anything, I really think you've been hanging out with Tori too long."

"Ooooooh, remind me not to keep you waiting again," I shot back.

"Maybe I will," he said.

Getting into the city was not a problem, but finding a parking space was a different matter. I was amazed that people parked in those tight spaces every day. Eventually we gave up on finding a space to park on the street and found a parking garage. It was really expensive and I offered to help pay, but Chris said he thought he could swing it.

We walked two blocks south to the coffee house. I checked my watch as we walked in. There was about fifteen minutes until the band went on. I asked the host if we could be seated in a corner table near the back, explaining to Chris that James was more comfortable performing when he didn't see people he knew right in front of him.

After the waiter took our order, I noticed that Jules was starting to fidget. It was a sure sign that she was getting nervous for James. She wasn't the only one. James was introducing 'our' song that night. I had never told anyone about the song, and I had my fingers crossed that everyone would like it.

I glanced at Chris and saw him looking around the room with interest. Everything in the room was in soft shades of brown, from beige to dark chocolate, and had a bohemian vibe going on. Following his gaze, I said to him, "Thanks for bringing us here tonight. My parents would never have let me come otherwise."

He turned his brilliant blue eyes back on me and gave me a lazy smile. His voice had an edge to it, though, when he said, "That's me, Mr. Safety."

"What do you mean?"

"Shhh," he said, "the show's starting."

The guys played about five or six cover songs, and then James stepped to the mike and said, "Our next song is a new one. We don't have a title yet, but we hope you enjoy it. The cowriter is here tonight and this performance is dedicated to her." He didn't identify me, which I was totally thankful for because I'd hate for people to hear it and know my most personal and painful moments.

James sang the verses and then on the chorus Noah joined in, and their harmony was really haunting. When the song was over the room was quiet. *Oh no, they hated it.* Then after about four seconds the room exploded into applause. A few people even stood. I was glad for James, but I was too busy trying to discreetly wipe the tears from my eyes to really enjoy the moment.

When their set was over the guys joined us at the table. James looked at me curiously. I was sure he wanted to let everyone know that I was the cowriter. I tried to give him a subtle signal, shaking my head just once, and James was wise enough to let the moment pass.

I put my game face on and did my best to enjoy the rest of the evening. Jules and James seemed to be getting along like they'd known each other forever and Tori was more than happy to keep the other members of the band entertained. It turned out the boy in the band from St. Benedict's knew Chris, or at least knew of him. Probably most people from St. Benedict's did, and I thought the boy was surprised that Chris was not full of himself like a lot of star athletes seemed to be.

I heard him asking Chris about colleges and I realized that Chris was in the same position my brother had been a year ago, so I kind of tuned into the conversation.

Chris said, "I didn't commit in the early signing period. I'm waiting to hear from the Ivies. So I won't be making a decision for awhile."

"Where do you want to go?" I asked.

He looked at me playfully, "Can't tell you. It's a state secret. If you found out, I'd have to kidnap you until the announcement."

"You don't have a refrigerator big enough to keep me fed for that long," I said, grinning.

He pulled out his cell phone and gave it a little wave, "Yeah, but there's always delivery."

I made a face and noticed the other boy looking at us like it was one crazy conversation.

As we were getting up to leave, Chris turned to James, "The songwriter, you never introduced her."

"No, sorry, I didn't." Then James changed the subject, and that seemed to end the matter.

*     *     *

When we got to the car, Tori told me to get into the front seat since she knew I was freezing and could really use the heater going full blast. In the back, the twins started rehashing the night, reviewing every song they'd heard. I caught Chris glancing over at me, noting my silence, but my eyes were half-closed with the warmth of the car and the late night. When the topic of James' new song came up, my eyes flew open.

"Didn't he tell you where it came from?" Tori asked Jules.

"No, he just said the band was working on something new."

"Well, it's as good as any of their cover stuff. I think they should get it published," Tori said.

"I'll have him get right on it," Jules said, laughing.

I looked at Chris and saw that he was amused with his sisters' chatter. He must have felt my eyes on him because he glanced at me and winked. I smiled back at him with drowsy eyelids, and in a few moments I must have fallen asleep because I didn't even remember us crossing the Ben Franklin Bridge back into New Jersey.

"Jackie … Jackie, wake up sleepyhead."

I opened my eyes and found Chris leaning toward me, his face inches from my own.

"Oh, sorry," I said, blinking rapidly. I looked in the back seat and saw his sisters were asleep too.

He ruffled my hair, then turned and opened his door, "Come on. I'll walk you to your door." He was around to my side of the car before I could even get the door open. He took my hand and helped me out of the car. I must have seemed really out of it because he even put his arm around my shoulders as he walked me up the drive. I don't know, maybe he thought I was going to keel over or something, but I thought it was totally unnecessary as I could feel the cold air waking me up.

When we got to the door, I thanked him again for driving us. He looked at me in a different way than usual, and said quietly, "I really like your song, Jackie."

Before I could open my mouth, he turned on his heels and was rapidly walking back to his car. As I started to close the front door, I watched the car pulling away, and I wondered how he knew.

*    *    *

I got a chance to talk to James the following Monday when we were on our way to English. "Sorry I didn't say anything Saturday, the song was awesome."

"I figured you didn't want me to identify you as the writer," he said. He slowed his pace and put his hand on my shoulder. "Don't ever be ashamed of having such powerful feelings. They make for great writing and some terrific music."

"Maybe, but I'm not like you, getting up in front of people and opening up like you do."

"You have a lot of good things to say, Jackie. It's not like I'm trying to turn you into a songwriter or anything, it's just," he seemed to be searching for the right words, and then he continued, "I just think you have something to share with people, that's all."

I appreciated the compliment, but his words made me feel a little self-conscious, too, so I changed the subject, "So how did Sunday's performance go?"

"Good. The management says they are going to have us back in April. They just have to check their dates."

"I'm really happy for you guys."

He smiled, and then changed the subject when he said, "Chris Hanson seems like a nice guy."

"Oh yeah, I've known him for years. He's just like a big brother."

James looked at me, and said, "Right," under his breath so I could barely hear him.

# - 25 -

Spring was around the corner and lacrosse was coming to Northfield. I had played in an indoor hockey league for the last two winters, but once it was over I had been bored out of my mind. I was too antsy for softball, and running around a track was just not for me. I was definitely glad our school was adding a new sport.

I told everyone the fun I had catching and throwing the ball on the beach last summer, so a lot of girls from field hockey were curious. We learned that Ms. O'Donnell, our hockey coach from freshman year, would be in charge of the girls' program, so it made trying lacrosse a no-brainer.

There were a couple of our hockey buddies that we would miss in the spring. I had tried to talk Lindsay into playing, but since she had a shot at being a starting pitcher in softball, she didn't want to give it up. Becky played softball, too. She had already been a varsity starter as a freshman, and our area newspaper, The Courier Press, tapped her as one of the up-and-coming infielders in all of South Jersey. Sam, on the other hand, was working after school. She started almost as soon as hockey was over. Anna said Sam had to do it to help her family. It made me feel lucky that even though my mom wasn't crazy about all this sports stuff for me, I didn't have to work after school to help pay the bills.

\*　　\*　　\*

The opening day of lacrosse was freezing and most of practice was spent just trying to stay warm. Ms. O'Donnell kept us moving, which wasn't easy 'cause we had so many layers on we could hardly bend our arms and legs. The thing I liked best about the first day of lacrosse was – there was no timed run. I thought Ms. O'Donnell was pretty smart not wanting to lose players right off the bat by making them work too hard. It was probably best to let the players think the sport was all fun and games 'til you had them hooked. At least that's the way I figured it.

My mom had bought me another piece of sports equipment. I thought it might mean she was giving up the good fight into making me a beauty queen or something when she grudgingly took me to the Sports Authority to buy my first lacrosse stick. I picked out a neon green one to kind of match my eyes – I'm such a dork!

Tori was a natural at the game with her height and long legs. I thought she might have found her sport. After the first week she had asked her mother if she could go to a lacrosse camp in the summer. For Tori, that was a major commitment.

Kerry Roth, one of our sophomore field hockey goalies, and a freshman I didn't know yet, were going to be our goalies. I thought it was really good for Kerry, playing 'in goal' without Becky around. Maybe she could be the number one goalie in lacrosse 'cause I didn't think she'd ever beat out Becky in hockey. And I have to say I gave Kerry major kudos for standing there in the goal while someone threw balls at her face. It sure wouldn't be me. On some things, I was a major baby.

We loved being around our old coach again. Lacrosse was to be just a club program for the first year so Ms. O'Donnell had us practice just four days a week, and since we weren't traveling to games, we got home a lot earlier. And that was a good thing since Mr. Barrows was really loading on the literature stuff. There was a new book every two weeks, and then we had to critique the writing. What could you really say? Hey Will, about the seventh line you wrote in Act II, Scene 3 in *Romeo and Juliet*, a little weak don't you think?

Actually, I wasn't complaining, I really loved English, plus James always kept things interesting in our class. The boy was SMART, but in a good way; like, he even kept Mr. Barrows on his toes. No wonder he and Jules got along so well.

As the spring semester was well underway, I had one piece of awkwardness in my life that really bothered me. Kurt Evans came up to me in homeroom one day and asked me out. He said since Mitch seemed to be out of the picture maybe it could be him and me.

I didn't know what to say. I thought he wasn't being very loyal to Mitch, but maybe I was being ridiculous since neither one of us would probably ever see Mitch again. Then I remembered the party and how he stuck me with the beer. I knew he wasn't for me, so I told him, "Thanks, but, no." He said, "Okay," and then ignored me for the rest of homeroom.

*     *     *

In the beginning of April the weather started to turn and temperatures started teasing into the fifties and sixties. The band was getting their second chance at The Brown Door in Philly and this time the twins and I were going to a matinee performance. On Sunday we were going to be brave and take the train. Initially Chris was going to take us, but the twins told me he would be making his final college visit the same weekend. Then he'd be signing his national letter of intent right after that which meant he was committed to going to that school if they accepted him.

At first, we thought our parents wouldn't let us go on our own and we'd have to cancel on the boys, but we managed to convince them that now we were almost juniors we really needed to expand our travel horizons.

My mom dropped us off at the high-speed line and when we got out of the car and walked into the station, I felt like I was crossing into another country, and thought maybe I should check to see if I needed a passport. It was embarrassing to be such a little girl from the burbs. I knew we were in the city just a few months ago, but now the three of us were really on our own, and that was a big difference.

It took us about ten minutes to figure out how to buy our train tickets from a machine and I kept messing up at the turnstile, forgetting to grab my ticket again when it popped out of the slot. I guessed I was still light-years away from international travel. But I figured, small steps, one foot in front of the other, right?

Getting off the train, we decided to walk to the stores on South Street before we saw the band play. Let me just say that South Street was not like shopping at the mall. It had an edge that you couldn't get in look-alike chain stores. Sort of punk meets hip-hop with an occasional Goth feel mixed in here and there. The people we passed on the street were even more interesting than what we saw in the stores.

The three of us had a blast, though, walking around like we were so cool and did the city all the time. I didn't think we fooled too many people, though, since we nearly got run over twice stepping off a curb too soon.

Tired of the sights, we decided to grab something to eat, and spotted a little deli on the corner. We ordered some hoagies, and just when I was ready to dig into my sandwich, Tori said to me, "We've got a favor to ask you."

I looked up slightly annoyed. How could anyone interrupt someone's first bite? Besides, it was past my feeding time and my mouth was watering. I ignored her and started munching.

Tori glanced at Jules for some silent confirmation then went on, "Well, we think Chris is going to call you."

I was kind of surprised at that. I mean, I hadn't even seen him since we went to see the band, him being so busy with basketball and everything.

I kept on chewing.

Then Jules joined in, "Chris's senior prom is coming up next month. And ..."

"Look, here's the thing," Tori said, sounding impatient with her sister. "He was supposed to ask somebody from St. Benedict's, but before he could, two other girls asked him instead, and then it got all crazy, so finally he told them both he already had a date. He was stuck."

Then Jules took up the story. "So anyway, he knew this fictitious date couldn't be anyone from his school because everyone would know her, and so ..."

"We sort of suggested you," Tori said.

My sandwich fell out of my hands, falling apart on my plate. I frowned at the mess.

Tori grabbed my arm before I could say anything. "I mean think of it, it's not like a real date. You guys are good buddies and you wouldn't possibly cause any drama with the girls at his school. You can't believe how they're always after him."

Well, actually I could believe it, but I kept my silence on that one.

"I'd have to wear a dress," I said, and I could hear the whine, or maybe it was anxiety rising up in my throat.

"Does that mean you'll do it, Jackie?" Tori asked, excitedly.

"I don't know," I said, cautiously.

"It would help him out of a jam," Jules said. "And I think it wouldn't be so bad. I mean you both like to dance, right?"

A lot of things were going through my head. On the one hand I thought, dress shopping, makeup, heels. Yuck, a total negative! On the other hand, I would be helping out a friend, and he'd always been there for all of us.

"Okay, I'll do it," I sighed, feeling like I had just been tag-teamed by two master connivers.

The twins grinned at each other with relief like they'd just accomplished some big, complicated mission. Tori said, "But Jackie, here's the deal, you can't act like you know any of this when he calls. It would really embarrass him about the girls asking him to prom and all."

"Uh, okay." I could understand that a conversation like that would make things a little awkward.

"Okay, that's settled," Tori said, "and don't worry, we'll help you shop for a dress." She started to get up.

"Hey, I didn't finish my sandwich yet," I wailed.

"Oh right," Tori said, like she had forgotten why we were even here, and then she grinned at her sister. I would swear if I didn't know better they were giving each other a silent high-five just then.

*     *     *

Two days later I saw on the local news that Chris Hanson had made his college commitment. It showed a picture of him doing the actual signing with his parents standing proudly behind him. The next afternoon I stopped at the card store in town, found an appropriate congratulations card, wrote a few lines, and mailed it that night.

Around dinnertime on Friday my cell phone rang. It was Chris. "Hey, thanks for the card, Jackie."

"No problem, I think it's great," I said.

"Yeah, I'm staying on the East Coast and the school has great academics so I'm pretty psyched." His tone changed and I could hear some seriousness creeping into his voice, "So here's the thing, the year is almost over and my school is having a dance."

I had to be cool here, like act clueless, so I said, "Oh really, what kind of dance?"

"Senior prom, actually. It's the third Saturday in May. I'm wondering if you would like to go with me."

I wasn't going to play this out any longer. I didn't hesitate. I simply said, "Yes."

"Really, that's great." He sounded relieved, like maybe any girl would ever reject him. What was he thinking? He continued, "Don't worry. I'll make sure you have a good time."

"So, should I wear my old navy sweats or should I go out and buy some gold ones to honor your school colors? What do you think?"

"Jackie McKendry, you can wear anything you want."

So that was pretty much it. That's how I was going to a prom with probably the best catch in South Jersey. Of course what made it great was there were no emotional entanglements going on, just two friends having a good time. Now I just had to deal with a dress.

*     *     *

On Monday, Tori about screamed at me at lunch, "You're going, you're going!"

"Isn't that what I'm supposed to be doing?" I said, acting all innocent.

"But he didn't tell Jules and me 'til this morning. We were going crazy all weekend wondering when he was going to ask you."

"Ask what?" Ellen asked, puzzled.

James, turned from his conversation with Eric and "What's going on?"

"Jackie here is going with my brother to senior prom," Tori said, grinning from ear to

"What a surprise," James said, dryly

"Shut up, James," Tori said, and

"What?" I said, looking at T

"Don't pay any attention to James, the boy is just slow," Tori said, looking exasperated.

James laughed, looked at me and shook his head. Then he turned his back on us, and resumed his conversation with his band members.

"So what kind of dress are you going to get?" Ellen asked.

"I don't know." My eyes kind of clouded over with the thought. *How come everyone was excited about a dress, but me?*

"I'll take care of it," Tori said. "We'll go out and look at magazines tonight." Then she gave me a look like she was dissecting an earthworm in biology or something, but I could be just a little oversensitive and maybe got that wrong.

After dinner my mom had to go food shopping, so she dropped Tori and me at the drugstore where we started skimming through the magazine section. I was feeling overwhelmed.

"I think you should wear something short," Tori said. "I can't see you in tons of fabric … maybe you should be in gold or maybe a green. What do you think?"

"I think I should have just said no."

Tori's face started to get stormy. "Look, do you want to ˙k this for my brother?"

ᵒo, of course not." I was feeling guilty now. Chris de-
ᵗter than this, like probably a girl who lived to get
"Okay, I'll be good."

Yᵒ

ᵗened up. "We'll start shopping next weekend.
ᵒme, right?"

"It would take a tornado to stop her," I said, selecting the magazine I wanted my mom to see.

"Good, then it's a date," Tori said.

\*     \*     \*

The following Saturday morning, my mom, Tori, and I were on our way dress shopping. When we had picked up Tori, I asked Jules if she wanted to go, but she told me only if she was bound and gagged.

"I guess that's a no," I said. She just grinned and went back to eating her breakfast.

Our first stop was to be the mall, and if that didn't work my mom had a list of backup stores. There were two stores in the mall that carried formals. One dress Tori wanted me to try on had so many cutouts that it exposed more skin than any of my bathing suits. Other dresses were too tight or too loose or the colors washed me out. Some of the dresses plunged so far down in the front or so much in the back that I thought I would have to be wrapped in packing tape to stay in the thing.

*How can anybody dance in this stuff?*

By noon I was feeling depressed. Picking out a dress was not going so well and I was getting hungry. Mom saw th was fading fast. "Let's grab something to eat," she said we'll try the store in Collingswood."

Fortified, we walked into the little store and it was really cute. Fun music was playinnd background. A tiny lady came over and ught the deal about the prom. Instead of show the lady sat me down and asked me what I was most looking forwa about saying "the end" but figured that was probably not what she was looking for, so I told her some stuff.

Then she went in the back and brought out three dresses. They were all short. One was a pale olive strapless number, the next was shimmering gold with soft brown metallic flecks, and the third was ivory, which I didn't think would work for me, but looked surprisingly good when I tried it on.

Mom and Tori were doing the evaluating as I pranced around in each dress. The saleslady showed them how things would look when I was wearing the 'right stuff' underneath, which would be another store trip that I would have liked to have avoided.

"They all look lovely on you. What do you think, Tori?" Mom asked. I could tell Tori was leaning towards the green dress.

"But what would Chris like?" I asked. "I mean it's his prom and all."

"Oh, boys don't care about that," Mom said.

"Actually, I really think Chris would like the ivory dress on Jackie," Tori said after giving each dress her critical review.

The saleslady took all this in, then said, "Just one minute, I'll be right back." She came out in five minutes carrying a beautiful teal dress. "I just remembered this, it came in this morning. Try it."

I slipped it on and I knew without looking in the mirror it was the one. It felt right, the fabric so cool against my skin. I did a little twirl and peeked into the mirror. Mom got teary. "Jackie, it's beautiful." I decided it was a keeper, and told Mom I could handle the rest and "let's please just get it over with."

Tori and Mom seemed much more relaxed now the dress purchase was over, and I could tell they would humor me through the rest of the day. When we left Tori off she said, "Mrs. McKendry, after today I know I'm totally prepared for shopping with my own two-year-old someday." Mom laughed and told her she had been a real trooper.

When we got home I showed my purchases to Lizzie. She got this dreamy look in her eyes and I knew she was storing up fantasies that were going to drive Mom and Dad crazy someday.

# - 26 -

Spring slid by, a mix of rainy days and pale sunshine. But the Saturday of prom turned into a perfect copy of an early summer day. From my bedroom windows I looked out into our backyard blooming with the dozens of bulbs my parents had planted. Everything looked alive and happy. Suddenly I was not worried anymore about saying yes to Chris.

I'd done my part – getting the dress and shoes and all, and I could endure my mom helping with my makeup routine. I had already been informed by Tori about things like eye shadow, liner, and nail polish. Chris definitely was getting some 'A plus' effort from little Jackie McKendry, that's all I could say.

Trying to get to sleep the night before, I admit I did have thoughts of other dances and proms going on, maybe like in Texas and it made me sad to think of Mitch waiting excitedly at the bottom of the stairs for some Southern belle and not me. But I know that was being selfish. If we couldn't be together then I should be wishing him happy times. You could wonder what my problem was since I was going to a prom myself, but it was not for romance and that was the difference.

In the morning I'd put those thoughts behind me and my feelings for Mitch had been placed into some quiet part of my heart. I was ready for the day. My mom had made an appointment for me at her salon, the Serendipity Spa, to get my hair trimmed and nails done. I thought prom preparations seemed so lopsided. I mean all a guy had to do was rent a tux and take a shower. It didn't seem fair.

\*     \*     \*

When we got to the salon Mr. Johns, the owner, fluttered over me like it was my wedding day or something. I thought Mom must have been his favorite client the way he fussed. Sitting in the massage chair getting my pedicure, I noticed Emma Connors walk into the salon. She had been our class secretary last year and was just the biggest phony in the whole world. She had her eyes on Mitch for awhile 'til she realized it wasn't getting her anywhere. I guess you could say we didn't exactly have a strong bond going.

She spotted me and walked over, and with her sweetie-sweet, phony voice said, "Jackie McKendry, what are you doing here?"

"Getting ready to go out," I said, keeping an eye on my toenails being filed.

"Really, where are you going?" I knew she was probably thinking like a ball field somewhere or something. I **so** wanted to stick her with a pin and watch all her hot air escape.

Instead I said, "Umm, St. Benedict's is having a dance." I was dragging this out, making her work for it.

I could tell she was surprised, although she tried to hide it, sputtering "You mean the prom?" Not wanting to be outdone she said, "Me too. Who's your date?" I couldn't be sure, but I thought she was gritting her teeth when she asked.

"I don't know whether you know him or not, Chris Hanson," I said, giving her an offhanded smile like it was no big deal.

Her eyes were bugging out of her head. I loved it. *Thank you, thank you, thank you,* I sent a prayer of gratitude to the twins for inadvertently giving me this moment. I knew I would pay for my evil thoughts someday, but maybe not right then.

"Jackie McKendry," she said, her eyes narrowing, trying to figure how this could possibly be, "I wonder, how do you get all the gorgeous boys?"

I knew by how she said this that it was not meant as a compliment, but more of an indictment of my character. And if I wasn't sitting there getting my toenails all buffed up right about then, I thought I would have gotten up and slugged her.

Not finding anything to gloat about, Emma turned away, "Well, see you tonight I guess. I think my manicurist is ready." As she walked away, I thought that she'd better get her claws sharpened 'cause I had faced much tougher than her on the hockey field.

\*     \*     \*

Chris was coming for me at six-thirty and I wanted no teasing from him tonight. I planned to be ready on time. So by six o'clock everything that was going on was on, except for my dress. Mom was in the bathroom helping me with the extra makeup touches. Lizzie was peeking in every so often to spy on my progress. I thought my little sister was more excited than my mom, and that was saying something. At six-twenty I slipped on my dress. Mom came back from her bedroom and said, "I have something for you that you might like for the evening." She handed me a box and inside were earrings and matching necklace.

"Oh, Mom, they're beautiful, thank you. I promise to take good care of them." I put on the earrings and my mom helped me with the necklace. I glanced in the mirror, *Okay Tori, I think all your work has paid off.*

Shortly the doorbell rang and my mom and sister left me to go downstairs. Then I heard my mom call my dad to get the camera. I gave it thirty seconds, grabbed my purse, and took a deep breath.

I slowly came down the stairs to my waiting family and Chris, and I wondered for a moment if when he saw me he'd be sorry he asked me to be his date. My eyes quickly sought him out and I tried to gauge his reaction. His eyes met mine, and they seemed to spark with something that was hard for me to read. Then his face became sort of peaceful, like it was all good. He, of course, was very James Bond in his white tux. There was just no other way to describe him, and I would be the biggest hypocrite in the world if I did not say how happy I was to share this night with him.

"I'm a little disappointed, Jackie," he said, with what seemed like sadness in his voice. Then he grinned when he saw the concern slide across my face. "Where's the gold sweat suit?"

Realizing that he was teasing me, and that he was really okay with everything, I relaxed and fired back, "I'll be glad to go back up and change, you know."

He laughed and slid his arm around my waist. "Come on outside. I think your mom and dad want to take some pictures. Oh, but first, this is for you," he said.

I smiled up at him when I saw the box. Inside was a small white gardenia that I had requested when he had asked what I wanted for a corsage. It was beautiful.

My parents must have taken a hundred pictures. Some of our neighbors even came out to catch the action and I started to get embarrassed with all the attention. But then I thought that maybe it was all about Chris being there, him being a pretty famous athlete in the area, so I tried to stay on my best behavior.

When the cameras were finally put to rest, Chris apologized, saying we had to do more of the same at his house. We said good-bye to my parents, and I wondered how famous film stars did it, putting up with the paparazzi in their faces all the time saying "look this way, look this way, hold it." Right then I decided that living a life where no one wanted to take your picture was definitely the way to go.

*　　*　　*

As we were driving to his house, he kept glancing over at me.

"What?" I said, finally.

"My sisters are going to have apoplexy when they see you."

"Don't I look okay?" I asked, and I looked down at my dress, puzzled.

"You clean up real good," he laughed. Then as he gave me a long slow appraisal that made me blush from head to toe, he shook his head and said, "Jackie, I'm glad I'm going away to college soon because I don't think I want to see all the hearts you're going to break."

I don't think he had to say another word. It was just the nicest compliment a girl could get even if he just made it up, and now I was ready to meet the rest of the night head-on.

When we got to his house, the Hanson family went through the same routine as mine. During one shot of us with Chris's arm around me, his mother went off in a flurry of Italian. Whatever she said, it startled Mr. Hanson. Tori grinned at us both, but Jules kind of scowled. I wanted to ask Chris what his mother had said, but he just said we had to get going.

Driving to the hotel where the prom was being held, he said, "We could have gone in a limo with some of my friends, but I know you can't stay out all night so I thought it would be better like this."

I never thought about my two o'clock prom curfew as being a problem until now. Then I realized there was probably a lot to a prom besides the dance itself. I frowned, "I'm sorry, this is going to mess things up for you."

"Never think that. All that after-prom stuff is not important. Besides, if I want to go back out and do other things, I will."

"You sure?"

"Yep." He took my hand, gave it a squeeze, and then slowly let it go.

*　　*　　*

At first the ballroom was too much to take in. It was more pictures, introductions to his friends, and beautiful decorations everywhere. He seated us at a table with Dean Rickert and his date Kelly Cunningham, another senior, who seemed really nice. Most of the others were his other basketball buddies and girls from St Benedict's.

The dancing was already underway and the DJ rocked. The music was all good stuff and not some lame 'last year' kind of music. Sitting next to me I could feel Chris's leg start to tap. He was catching it. I turned to him, "So are you going to just sit there and waste this, or what?"

He laughed and grabbed my hand, "Come on. Let's see if you've still got it."

It had been a while, but I had to say when it came to dancing Chris and I still had it going on. I thought he was actually surprising some of his teammates so I didn't know how many times they'd seen him like this. I felt like we were right back in Washington Elementary, our old school, dancing on the beds in his sisters' room pretending to be background dancers in a music video. I was totally in my comfort zone.

After awhile I told him that I'd be right back and took off for the restroom. Washing my hands, I overheard some girls talking.

"Can you believe Chris Hanson is here?" one said.

"No, who'd he bring? No one from our school, right?" said another.

"I don't know, but she must be something. No one here has been able to pin him down for more than a few dates. There are a lot of disappointed girls out there tonight, that's for sure," the first girl said.

I gulped. All of a sudden I felt self-conscious as I slowly made my way back to our table. Chris noticed that I was awfully quiet. "What's the matter, Jackie?"

I didn't look at him and just shrugged my shoulders. I could tell he was puzzled and didn't know what had changed things.

"Say," he said, "how about a little feeding frenzy?"

"Okay," I said, and gave him a smile.

He said he'd surprise me and be right back. Dean joined him.

After he left, Kelly slid over to the seat next to mine. "Having a good time?"

"Sure," I said smiling back at her. She seemed so nice.

"Chris is a good guy. I've known him for two years now since Dean and I started dating." I leaned forward, glad to be distracted. She continued, "I'm glad Chris came to prom. His dad keeps him so busy, he hardly has any time for other things, you know." I nodded my head, and began to relax again. Then she said, laughing, "Do you know how many girls would die to be in your place?"

"I've been hearing that," and I looked down at the table feeling even more self-conscious than before.

She reached out and put her hand on mine. "Don't worry about it. Believe me, he's having a great time, I can tell, and that's the important thing."

She was right. That was all that mattered. I smiled back at her. "Thanks, Kelly."

A boy who was not from our table came up to us and spoke to Kelly. I figured she must know him, and then he turned to me and introduced himself to me as a friend of Chris's, and asked me to dance. I didn't quite know what the proper thing was, but since he was a friend of Chris's, I said "okay."

He walked me onto the dance floor. It was a slow song, something that Chris and I hadn't even danced to yet. He wrapped his arms around me possessively like he really knew me or something, and I began to feel a little uncomfortable.

"So," he said, "you're the girl with the brass ring." I must have looked confused, so he continued, "The one that snagged the great Chris Hanson. He indicated a table not too far away. "Your friend Emma over there says you're a hot one." I felt an IOU dancing across the floor to me, and I knew for sure that Emma and I would go to war someday.

He started sliding his hand lower on my back. "How about when you and Chris are done, you let me give you a little call." His hand was definitely moving into dangerous territory now, and I tried to struggle and pull away, but he was gripping me tightly.

All of a sudden, his hand was ripped away, and in a flash Chris had twisted the boy's arm behind his back.

The boy grunted, "You're hurting me."

"Apologize," Chris hissed.

"Sorry," the boy said, only because he was forced to.

"Mean it," Chris said between clenched teeth.

The boy looked into my eyes, all his insolence gone now, and said, "I'm sorry."

"Now get lost Zac, before I tear your freakin' head off," Chris growled in a low voice.

"Okay, okay," the boy said hurriedly as he rubbed his arm. Then he turned away, and was quickly swallowed up in the crowd.

Chris slid his arm around me without missing a beat, took my hand, and started moving us to the music. I took a quick glance around. Apparently, the little drama had gone unnoticed by those around us.

"Are you okay?" Chris said gently.

I just nodded. I was stunned at what had just happened.

"He's a creep. I should have never left you."

I didn't want this to spoil the night for Chris so I said, "No. Don't feel that way. I'm okay, really," and I smiled up at him.

We let the dreamy music wrap around us and we both started to calm down. The dance floor was packed by now. This music must have been putting everyone in the mood. After a moment I got bumped by some exuberant couple. The movement pushed me up against Chris's chest. I started to pull back but Chris kept me locked against him.

"The floor is just a little crowded, Jackie."

I let out a sigh and turned to rest my cheek against his chest. I heard him humming softly, in his funny out of tune way, and I relaxed entirely, giving myself up to the moment and enjoying it all.

The rest of the night continued on. It was just about the two of us having fun with each other and his friends. Riding home in the car, his arm around the back of my seat, he looked at me and asked, "Sleepy?"

I nodded dreamily, "Past my bedtime."

"Have fun?"

I closed my eyes and whispered, "Yes, tons."

When we got to my house, he walked me to the door, and I thought what a wonderful night it had been and what a good time we've had together.

He stopped at my door. The night had been terrific, far better than I could have imagined. I turned to him and impulsively reached up and wrapped my arms around his neck and kissed him on the cheek. I began to thank him for inviting me, but instead I felt his body grow still.

*Oh no, I shouldn't have done that. I've crossed the line and now he's mad.* I stepped back, and my eyes started to tear.

He gave a little smile and said, "Sorry – you startled me." His eyes were resting on my mouth, and he reached up and slid his thumb softly across my lower lip.

"Do you know that you have the most inviting mouth, Jackie McKendry?"

I felt him lean toward me. I barely breathed, expecting a quick good-night kiss. Instead, his fingers slowly slipped down to the pulse thumping away in my throat. Then he whispered, "But I'll wait … until it's me you really want to kiss."

With that he turned, and whistling tunelessly, walked quickly down the path to his car. I didn't move for a full thirty seconds. I was really not sure what had happened. I was just relieved to know he wasn't mad at me about the kiss and all. Then I walked into the house, my first perfect prom night over.

# - 27 -

The spring semester was coming to a close, and I could feel the pull of summer vacation. Everyone was counting down the days until school was over. But in those few remaining days several things happened that got me thinking of the future.

It started with the grand finale of our first season of lacrosse. I couldn't get over what a crazy, fun sport it was. It was faster than hockey, and you could go around the back of the goal cage to set up plays. Of course we didn't have any plays, but Ms. O'Donnell said we would someday. The wildest part was every time the whistle blew you had to stand still, and then you couldn't move 'til the ref blew the whistle again. That sure took some getting used to.

We were now getting to a point where we could actually string three passes together before someone dropped the ball, so we were excited when Ms. O'Donnell announced we would be ending the season by having a play day with two other schools that were starting lacrosse like us.

Jules was playing defense and let me say with her size and reach she was sure hard to get around. Tori and I were midfielders, which meant we went both on attack and defense. It was a lot of running. I figured it would keep us in great shape for hockey. Most of the girls had stayed with the lacrosse club all spring, so next year Northfield would have a regular JV schedule, and the following year we'd go varsity.

I was excited to be part of a sport from the beginning. It kind of felt like being a pioneer. Like maybe someday I would come back to Northfield and find the lacrosse team as great as the hockey team and I could say I helped get things rolling. I flashed forward in my head and thought that summer would be filled with throwing lacrosse balls against our garage door and dribbling hockey balls around our driveway. Maybe I could alternate balls like a juggler, and go on television with my special talent. Or then again, my mom might send me off to some deprogramming center where they'd try to knock all of the sports nonsense right out of me. Fat chance!

*    *    *

The following week, Mrs. Fortunato called all the returning hockey players together for an after-school meeting in one of the health rooms. First, she went over all our plans for going to a hockey camp in Virginia. She wanted us to try a new place because she liked us to be exposed to a lot of different coaches. Then she gave us our training program. It looked pretty tough and we all moaned and groaned when we saw it, but she paid us no mind.

The final part of the meeting was a bit of a surprise. At the end of the fall season, Coach had us fill out peer evaluation forms where your teammates anonymously rate you on certain things like listening skills, work habits, commitment, and stuff like that. Everyone was supposed to take it seriously.

Mrs. Fortunato told us she had summarized the results and included her own thoughts in a letter she was handing out to us. She asked us to think about what was written as we were getting ready for next season.

I turned the sealed envelope round and round in my hand wondering what was inside, but we weren't to read them 'til we got home.

Coach also used this information to pick captains. We didn't vote like some teams did. Instead, she went through what was written about the players and figured out captains on her own. I guessed that was how Mandy was picked last spring.

She told us we were having two captains next season. The first was Kate Carson, which was no surprise. Then she named the second. It was Jules. Tori reached over to her sister and gave her a hug. Everyone clapped. Well, almost everyone. Lindsay didn't, and that was no surprise either.

I felt myself clapping, but my mind was flying forward. I wondered if being named a captain would change my friend. Maybe she'd have no time for me 'cause she would be so busy with the team. The thought unsettled me. I watched people crowding around Kate and Jules, gave myself a mental slap, and then got up to offer my congratulations.

*     *     *

On Friday, Mom had to do some errands and took Lizzie and me with her. She dropped me off at the grocery store with a short list of items to get while she went to the library with Lizzie. I picked up most of the groceries and was going down the last aisle to get the milk when I heard behind me, "Jackie McKendry, is that you?"

The color drained from my face. I knew that voice. I turned. It was Mitch's dad, Major Kennedy.

He smiled broadly. "How are you, honey?"

I quickly scanned behind him to make sure he was alone. My voice sounded kind of wooden to me, and I was sure my smile didn't quite reach my eyes when I said, "Fine sir, and you?"

He didn't miss my reaction and he said more carefully, "Good, retired now as of a week ago."

"That's great," I said, but a thousand questions were fighting to get out ... *What does this mean? Where's your family? How's Mitch?*

"Can I tell my son I saw you?" he asked.

I shrugged my shoulders, "Sure." To be polite I added, "How is he?"

"Better now, it's been a long year, though. Well, I need to get going. It's been good to see you. Please tell your parents I said hello." Then he moved on past me.

I remained in the aisle for another few minutes, partly because I was too stunned to move and partly because I didn't want to face Mitch's dad again. There was too much going on inside my head.

As I slid into the front seat of our car, Mom asked, "What took you so long? You only had to get a few things."

"I ran into somebody in the store ... Major Kennedy."

I must not have looked too good 'cause my mom reached for my hand and gave it a squeeze.

She got it. She did know how much I was hurt when Mitch left. I told her Major Kennedy had retired and I know she wanted to ask me more, but she didn't say anything. She just kept her focus on the road.

It took a day or two to get myself back on an even keel. I thought it was mostly the surprise of Mitch's dad and being reminded of the past that got me so down. I decided if I saw him again I would be much better with it.

\*     \*     \*

The week's finale was Chris Hanson's graduation party. When my brother finished high school my mom and dad took him out to dinner and gave him a nice gift, but the Hansons did things way differently. It was going to be a big event. Mrs. Hanson's mother, the twins' nana, was coming over from Italy and their dad's parents were flying in from California. Mr. and Mrs. Hanson had also invited their important business associates, as well as their friends.

When my family arrived I saw Chris standing in the midst of all these people, everyone fussing over him. He spotted me and rolled his eyes, like, what can you do? Parents! I gave him a big grin and thumbs up. Someone grabbed his attention and he smiled at me before he turned back to answer whatever was asked of him.

The food was delicious and the spirits were flowing. At one point his nana came over to me, and patted me softly on the cheek. She said in halting English, "The pretty girl from the pictures ... good, good." I thought she was under the impression that Chris and I were together or something. I looked into her eyes that were gazing back at me with such tenderness and I simply didn't have the heart to correct her.

I didn't ever really have much of a chance to talk to Chris at the party. He was definitely the evening's prince in everyone's eyes. And that was okay. He gave me a night I'd never forget and I wished him the very best as he got ready for college. I knew from watching my brother this year that there was no looking back for Chris, and there shouldn't be.

\*    \*    \*

Finally, the last day of school was over and we were free at last. I was cleaning out my desk, tossing all the unneeded papers from tenth grade on the floor. The whole thing put me in a reminiscing mood. I reached into my file drawer and pulled out the calendar that had been hanging above my desk the year before. Thumbing through the pages I came to August and smiled at the large red star circling the day I left for camp. My mind drifted through all the days that followed.

I thought of my indecision about trying to make the varsity and being so scared of what other people would think. Then there was Mitch getting yanked out of school and both of us not being able to do anything about it. I think I kind of lost myself for awhile.

Right then and there, I decided that getting through sophomore year deserved another star. I figured I had earned it for stepping up, and finding some direction when everything in my life seemed so messed up. Of course, I wouldn't tell anybody about the star. It's not like it was something I could show off on a refrigerator door.

I was going to toss the calendar, adding it in with my other discards scattered across the floor, then changed my mind and shoved it back in the drawer. Starting to go downstairs I glanced at my desk one more time. I was thinking – *I might need that old calendar next fall. It'll be a reminder of the time I was lost and got myself found – the year I made varsity.*

# The End

# Acknowledgments

Once I created the characters in **Freshman Season**, my challenge was to keep them alive so their story could continue. Like Jackie McKendry, I had a team behind me all the way. They were a group of people who had my back and cheered me on through the rough spots so that I could realize my dream.

A special thanks goes to my readers Beth McGinnis, Tricia Marino, MacKenzie McGuckin, and Casey Hanna for their time and suggestions. They had a huge impact in shaping the story. My biggest shout-out goes to Sarah Keller who edited the book with such diligence and good humor. She certainly earned her own varsity letter, and now knows more about the sport of field hockey than she could have ever imagined.

CPSIA information can be obtained at www.ICGtesting.com
Printed in the USA
BVOW02s0137240114

342849BV00009B/175/P